ERIN

CLOVER SPRINGS MAIL ORDER BRIDES 9

RACHEL WESSON

LONDONGATE PUBLISHING

CHAPTER 1

NEW YORK, MAY 1887

"You can come in now Mrs. Cooper."

Erin pushed her hair back, trying to calm her nerves. She took a quick look in the mirror to make sure she was presentable before moving from the waiting room into the larger room.

Three doctors were sitting at the main desk in front of her. She wasn't asked to take a seat. That was the first bad sign. She made a mental note to remember how hard this was. Next time she had to deliver news to a patient she would try being more understanding. That is if there was a next time.

The doctor sitting in the middle looked up from his notes, pushing his thin framed glasses up on the bridge of his nose. "There is no easy way to say this, Mrs. Cooper."

"Just tell me straight, Sir, please."

"We have read the court papers and have debated this issue most strenuously. I would like to congratulate you on your achievements while working at the hospital. If circumstances were different, I believe you would have made an excellent doctor."

"You mean if I had been a man?"

"Now there is no call for that attitude." The most senior doctor on the panel said. His condescending tone and the fact he stared at a point over her head told her, her fate was sealed.

"When do I have to leave?"

She crossed her fingers hoping they would allow her to sit her final examinations. It was a long shot but…

"Today."

Despite not being asked to sit down, Erin sat. She was afraid her legs would buckle under her and she had some pride left.

"I believe, I thought there was the opportunity for an appeal?" she said, her voice not as clear and steady as she would have liked.

"The circumstances, in this case, require a final decision. Mrs. Cooper, your presence here is a distraction. You must leave these premises immediately. Your things will be collected and delivered to your home."

"But I was proved …"

"Our decision is final. Good day, Mrs. Cooper."

Erin stood up in a haze. She must have looked shocked as the doctor who had first addressed her, stood and held the door open for her. "Erin, I am sorry. I tried," he said quietly. "Is there someone waiting for you at home?"

"No, Doctor. Thank you for your time. Good day."

She wasn't completely surprised although she'd hoped her reputation and hard work would count for more. Thank goodness Mam had already sailed. She didn't need this news on top of everyone else.

She couldn't remember getting home. Pushing the door open, she was glad Mrs. Doherty, her housekeeper, was still there. She'd make her a cup of tea before she left for the day.

"Why you are so white? Did you have more trouble?"

"I am fine Mrs. Doherty. I walked a little too quickly is all. I would love a cup of tea if you would be so kind."

"Will I put a drop of whiskey in it for you, lass? My doctor swears by it you know."

Erin did know. She came up against this on a daily basis. So many doctors prescribed alcohol to their patients in the dim hope it would make them feel better. Perhaps it did but only for the short term.

"No thank you, Mrs. Doherty. A cup of tea would be just fine."

Mrs. Doherty went off muttering something but Erin didn't take any notice. She wanted to sit down and rest for a while before she started looking at her financial affairs. This house would have to go. She had a small sum of cash saved up and some pieces of jewelry she no longer wanted. She could sell them but would it be enough? She wanted to give Mrs. Doherty a couple of months wages to tide her over till her next job. Housekeeper positions were difficult to find given the huge number of young immigrants arriving on a daily basis. She would, of course, give her a wonderful reference but after today, how much weight would that hold? Mrs. Doherty may be better off lying than to admit to working for her.

* * *

A COUPLE of weeks later the house was sold together with most of her possessions. The house had been heavily mortgaged so after paying back the debt and providing for Mrs. Doherty, she was left with very little cash.

Mrs. Doherty had cried bucketfuls when Erin told her she had to leave New York. The poor woman had even invited Erin to come to share her house rather than going west and being alone amongst strangers. Touched as she was at the gesture, Erin knew her housekeeper couldn't afford to feed another person.

Erin was nearly as badly off financially. She looked at her total worldly goods. A few items of clothing, her medical books, and instruments. Her most prized possession was her uncle's medical bag, the leather weathered from years of use but you could still see the initials E Brennan MD. Her pa's younger brother had married a wealthy widow some years older than him. She had supported him through medical school. She got a charming young handsome doctor on her arm and he got the chance to make a dream come true and practice medicine. Despite the age difference, they were very happy together.

When they died in a train derailment, she'd been surprised to find her uncle had not only left her a small allowance but his medical bag and books. The bulk of their estate went to the son of her uncle's wife. He'd never approved of his mother's remarriage so there was no help from that quarter.

Mam had gone back to Ireland but before she left, she had asked Erin to bring a gift to Father Molloy. She wanted to thank him for all the things he had done for the family over the years. Erin couldn't understand why her mam didn't just post it but Mam had insisted it be delivered in person. She mentioned something about a dream she had but Erin didn't pay much notice. Her mam laid great store by what she called her gift. She reckoned she had the second sight. Erin didn't believe anyone could see Dain to the future never mind her mam. If she could, surely she would have foreseen what happened to her da. He was a fireman and had been killed trying to help a family escape a high rise. Erin didn't want to think about her da, not now. Not ever. He hadn't wanted her to become a doctor. They'd argued and were not speaking when he died.

Her mam had supported her every step of the way. When everyone else laughed at the idea of a woman becoming a doctor, Mam had given them her look. Mairead Brennan's look could stop a train. Or so the locals used to say. Nothing stopped her mam when she got an idea in her head.

She wondered what her mam would think of her heading out west. But then what choice did she have? Nothing could have made her stay in New York. Despite the size of the city, gossip spread fast. She would never get used to people staring at her in the streets or cutting her dead.

Erin sat on the train, her things in a small carpet bag with the medical bag on her knee. A couple of people glanced at the bag. She shared the same initial as her uncle. If she was going to start a new life alone, she might as well shake off the baggage of her previous one. Everything could go starting with her name. No more Mrs. Cooper. From now on, she answered to Erin Brennan.

CHAPTER 2

CLOVER SPRINGS

Mick Quinn pushed the hat back from his eyes. He was looking forward to seeing the people of Clover Springs again. He felt more at home here than anywhere else he had ventured on his travels. Cookie liked it too otherwise he wouldn't have come with him. Despite his grumbling, the man enjoyed staying at the Sullivan ranch. Mick wondered if he had a thing for Mrs. Higgins. Not that he would ask. They may be very good friends but Cookie was almost like a father to him. And there was one thing you didn't ask your pa about and that was his love life.

Mick hoped being surrounded by old friends would help him shake his melancholy. Every year he traveled back to the farm hoping for good news. As usual, he had gone this year only to be disappointed again. The Stevensons, who rented the farm and were doing an amazing job, were always friendly and hospitable but he felt uncomfortable at the pity he saw in their eyes. Why he had ever shared his story, he didn't know. He usually didn't tell anyone. Perhaps it was the concern Mrs. Stevenson expressed. She'd known him for nearly twenty years and kept telling him it was time to put down roots, meet a nice girl and have a family of his own. Ha! Little did she know the war hadn't only robbed him of his past but his future too.

"You going to sulk all day? "Cookie said as they got nearer the Sullivan ranch.

"I ain't sulking. I was thinking is all."

"Listen, son, I been meaning to say this for some time. I think we should stop returning to Virginia every year. Don't go looking at me like that. I ain't saying there's no hope but the Stevensons would send you a telegram if they found out anything."

"It's not the same."

"No, it ain't but it sure beats the heartache you bring on yourself. Visiting that old place, all those memories. It ain't good for you. You know it and I know it. Ain't good for nobody. Some things are best left in the past."

"Cookie, I ..."

"I know you don't want to hear it but think on it, please. I only got your best interests at heart."

Cookie set his horse into a gallop in the direction of the ranch. Mick followed behind not giving into his horse's desire to run too. Was Cookie right? Should he give up now, after all these years? He stared into the distance not seeing the large Sullivan ranch but another small farm, a lady pulling water from the well, a man checking his horse and two little...... Enough. Cookie's right. Looking back isn't helping anyone.

"Mick, welcome back. We thought we'd have to send out a search party when you didn't arrive last week. You missed the Harvest Festival and all," Davy Sullivan greeted him.

"I know I'm late, Davy. Had some stuff to sort out. How are things here? How's the missus and that fine baby of yours?"

"Mary is great, not sure anyone would love Cathy at the moment. She got her ma's Irish temper."

Mick laughed. Mary Sullivan wasn't your average Irish woman. She had a nice calm temperament provided she wasn't too upset. She could talk forever but getting all fired up quickly wasn't her style. He wasn't about to sing her virtues to his boss though. Although they had got over the mix up over the birthday present that first year Mrs. Sullivan had come to live in Clover Springs, he didn't want to push his luck. Davy was protective over his Mrs. Rightly so given the shortage of women in the area.

"Any trouble since we been gone?" Mick asked.

"None. At least not on the ranch."

Mick looked at his boss more closely. Something was up.

"You heard there's been more trouble with the sheep herders? Not with my men, they know I won't stand for it. But that doesn't mean it won't spill over onto my land."

"So what's with the frown?" Mick asked.

"You will find changes in Clover Springs. The men were pleased to see a new house open up."

"A house?" Mick clarified.

"You know the type I mean. They don't hold quilting parties or sewing bees."

"A bordello in Clover Springs? How did that one get past Mrs. Grey and the rest of the townsfolk." Mick saw Davy's frown. "What ain't you telling me, boss?"

"Mick, I know single men got to have their entertainment but this house, it isn't right. The women, well they are only girls really... You know what I'm trying to say."

"Have you told the men its off limits?"

Surprised Davy stared. "No, I can't do that. They may be my workers but I ain't their Pa. They got to make their own decisions. But I sense trouble brewing. Dickinson, he's the owner. He reminds me of Coleman - that man who tried to take Laura away. He has shifty eyes."

"Do you want me to do something in particular?" Mick was still a little confused as to why Davy was telling him all this.

"Just watch yourself, Mick. I know you have a hot temper particularly when it comes to women and kids. I don't expect you to stand by if anyone is being mistreated but when it comes to Dickinson and his men, you might not want to handle it alone. That's all I'm saying." Davy looked at him. Mick nodded.

He understood Davy's warning and was more than a little touched by the fact he cared enough to make it. They sure had come a long way since the first year Mary Sullivan had arrived.

"Come on, Mrs. H will have my head. She's baked a feast. She said she had a feeling you'd be back soon and got prepared."

"Sure, that's the only reason I come back to Clover Springs. Mrs. Higgins's cooking."

Mick gave his horse to one of the boys who helped the ranch hands with the chores. "After his rubdown, give him plenty of oats, he's earned it."

The boy led his horse away. Mick walked toward the kitchen spotting Cookie laughing and joking with

Mrs. H. They did look like a couple. He wondered if he might just have a word with Aaron and Samuel. With the boys both being relatively newlyweds, they might just convince their Ma to give it a go with Cookie. She wouldn't get a better man that was for sure.

CHAPTER 3

"Morning Wilma." Father Molloy walked into the orphanage closing the door behind him.

"Did you smell the cookies? I just baked a new batch this morning. I have to wait till the children go to school or they eat them all as soon as they come out of the oven." Wilma chuckled.

Father Molloy knew she didn't mind the children taking the cookies in the slightest. After what those little ones had been through, they deserved cookies every day as far as she was concerned.

He took a seat at the table.

"Is Ellen down at the school too with baby Jake?"

Wilma frowned. "Yes, she is and you need to have a word with that woman. She be doing too much. She should be resting after a difficult birth. Stubborn as a mule she is."

"You would know more about that than me, Wilma."

Wilma laughed. "I don't know about that Father. You can be more stubborn than Miss Ellen and me put together." Her tone grew more serious. "I'm telling you though she ain't listening to nobody. Laura is trying to persuade her to take more time off, but Miss Ellen thinks there are too many children for one teacher."

"Ellen is right. There are." Catching the look on Wilma's face, Father Molloy quickly continued. "Ellen shouldn't be there though, not with her still feeling so ill. I will speak to Mrs. Grey. She seems to have a way of talking Ellen around."

"I was talking to Miss Alicia, I mean Alicia last week about the children."

Father Molloy noticed her slip but didn't comment. It would take Wilma a long time to stop calling white folk mister and miss, despite Alicia's insistence she treat them as her equal.

"You know I am still rather shocked, but delighted, you two have become such good friends."

"Me and Alicia? Me too. If you had told me that day she arrived in Clover Springs, she would fast become like family to me, I would have said you done lost your mind."

"God works in mysterious ways," Father Molloy said half teasing as he knew Wilma hated it when he referenced God like that.

"I don't know about God and mysterious ways, but I do know you be a good judge of character. You saw something in Alicia that day or you wouldn't have invited her to Clover Springs."

Father Molloy didn't confirm or deny her assumption.

"Is she back from her trip yet?"

"They is all due home tomorrow. I can't wait to see her, Aaron and those two sweet boys of theirs. Mr. Aaron, he was kicking up a big fuss because Alicia told him he had to wear a fancy suit to their meeting. You should have heard him complaining to Mr. Samuel about it. He was saying he not one of those city boys." Wilma was laughing so hard, her whole body wobbled. She wiped the tears of laughter from her eyes.

"I hope the visit proves successful."

"You mean you hope Alicia shows more tact than she did when she first came here."

Father Molloy nodded, not surprised she had read him so well. "A lot of people don't take too kindly to women bosses, particularly those who are likely to complain if the workers aren't being treated too well."

"Well, I guess Alicia has learned a few things. Part of

her making Aaron dress nicely was so they would assume he be the boss. But woe betides them if she finds bad working conditions for the miners or worse children working in her mine. The men in charge will be out on their butts quicker than you can say jack rabbit."

"Quite right too," Father Molloy agreed. "I wonder if the Higgins will continue to live here in Clover Springs or move nearer to the mine."

"Leave Clover Springs? Over my dead body is they going up them mountains. No fit place for young boys to grow up surrounded by miners. They need their friends, their school and..."

'Their Wilma with baked cookies." Father Molloy knew Wilma had taken the orphans to her heart just as much as she had taken Alicia. He hoped for her sake Alicia and Aaron decided to stay on the homestead. They could afford to live in luxury anywhere they wanted once they had been married twelve months. They would gain full control of Alicia's inheritance then.

"Alicia is coming back. We been talking and she wants to use some of her money to make Clover Springs even better. We need to find another teacher and build a bigger school and ..." Her voice trailed off. Surprised she had stopped in full flow, Father Molloy looked up.

"You look tired, Father. Why are you not sleeping? What you worried about now? The Red Feathers?"

"Wilma, this is why I come to see you, to talk. You seem to read my mind better than most anyone else. I admit I am very concerned."

Wilma took a seat, resting her chin on her hands as she gave him her full attention. He sighed as he tried to frame his thoughts in the least judgmental way possible.

"I know some men like to have a drink. And I know they have certain..." he trailed off unable to find the words.

'They got an itch that needs to be scratched," Wilma supplied making him smile

"Not sure I would put it quite like that but yes. I want everyone to feel welcome in Clover Springs. But I don't believe we need something like that establishment. I want to find a way to close it down but without a huge fuss. I do not want to embarrass the men who visit the house, but more importantly the women who work there."

Wilma stared at him for a couple of seconds.

"That's what makes you different from a lot of religious men. Some of the clergymen I've encountered would have spoken out against any man who frequented the Red Feathers from the altar at services. "

"Well, I might have been tempted to say a few words about the owner," Father Molloy admitted reminding himself he should find a confessor. But that could wait until he sorted out this latest problem.

"What can I do to help you?" Wilma asked.

"I was wondering if you had spoken to the ladies, the ones working there." Father Molloy pulled at his collar, it felt very tight all of a sudden.

Wilma gave him a knowing look. "You know I have, Father. I made it my business to show those girls they have a friend in Clover Springs if they ever need a shoulder to cry on. Makes me sick to my stomach to see how some folk treat them. Some people do need to concentrate more on your sermons."

Father Molloy's mind went blank. He looked at her for an explanation.

"You know those ones where you can't judge other people and we should all love one another. See I have been listening."

"Now don't you get all fired up on me, Wilma."

"I ain't gettin' fired up." Wilma stared at him and then shrugged her shoulders. "Okay, maybe a little. It's only they be so young. I was telling Miss... I mean Alicia there is one girl who reminds me of Tilly, the orphan you both rescued on the train. Mollie, the girl from the Red Feathers only be about a year or so older than Tilly."

Father Molloy struggled to keep his temper under control. It was one thing for ladies in their twenties to be working in these establishments, it was quite another for young girls to be forced into that line of work. There was no doubt in his mind they hadn't become a woman of the night out of choice.

"You tried talking to the sheriff?" she asked.

"Yes, but his hands are tied. Dickinson hasn't broken any laws, least none which we know about."

"You bet he has done all sorts of things," Wilma said. "Men like him, they don't care about no laws. All they see is dollar signs."

Father Molloy saw Wilma fighting back tears. He could only imagine the horrors this brave beautiful woman had seen in her lifetime. He was sorry he had brought back bad memories but the reality was he needed Wilma's help. There was no way he could get the Red Feather ladies to speak to him as they would to Wilma.

"Why they let him open that house here anyway?" Wilma's angry tone highlighted her frustration, "We should have stopped that happening as soon as he took his dirty a..."

Father Molloy coughed just in time. Wilma gave him a grin before she corrected herself, "feet out of the train and said he was staying. He looked like an oily rat right from that first day."

"Mrs. Shaw thought he was charming. As indeed did Miss Hawthorn. He even tried to charm Mrs. Grey," Father Molloy said.

"Well, Lorena Ella Grey didn't fall for his pitter patter and neither did I. As for those other two ladies, do you think we could convince Dickinson to take them with him when he does leave?"

Despite himself, Father Molloy laughed. "Wilma you are going to get me into trouble for agreeing with sentiments like that. I will pray on it."

"You do that Father. Maybe another wedding might happen. Mr. Dickinson could marry Miss Hawthorn and live happily ever after somewhere else. Australia might be far enough."

Father Molloy left the orphanage with a smile on his face. The situation with Dickinson had troubled him no end. He felt better after talking with Wilma. He mostly always did.

CHAPTER 4

Mick finally got the opportunity to visit the town. He wanted to see the Red Feathers for himself. It was located right next to the saloon and it'd been some time since he had a decent drink. Cookie didn't like alcohol so it was pointless trying to get him into a saloon when they were traveling.

He tied his horse to one of the hitching posts and walked down the street toward the saloon. Even if you didn't know the Red Feathers existed, nobody could claim they didn't know from looking at it the type of house it was. The building itself was painted bright red with what he supposed were white feathers painted here and there. It would have looked out of place in most towns but particularly in the quiet town of Clover Springs. As he walked by, a couple of scantily clad ladies came out onto the veranda.

"New in town cowboy? My name's Lily. What's yours?"

Mick didn't answer her question, he simply nodded in acknowledgment as he walked by.

"You ever get lonely sugar, you be sure to call in. I know how to put a smile on your face," Lily said as he passed. "I'll join her," another girl called out.

Mick had been to some disreputable towns but even he was shocked by how forward Lily and her friends were. He wondered what Father Molloy and Reverend Timmons made of them. Pushing the door of the saloon open, he headed inside. Davy had given him the warning to watch himself but he hadn't said anything about Mick trying to find out more. If there was anywhere in town where he'd find the information he needed, it was from Gary the barkeep at the saloon.

Instead of Gary, a new face stood behind the bar. He wore a sullen expression and seemed to think paying customers were a hindrance. Mick looked around.

"Where's Gary?"

"Who's asking?"

"Me," Mick answered staring at the barkeep. He

wasn't about to be intimidated by the scrawny little upstart.

"Gary left town. He had people to see."

That was odd. Gary had no family and was quite happy in Clover Springs. The presence of the saloon was accepted by the majority of the townsfolk because Gary was an honest man. He didn't allow girls or gambling and closed up every Sunday. Some had said they'd seen him in Church. The barkeep was lying but why.

Mick decided now was not the time.

"Don't matter none. I guess I'll catch up with him the next time I'm visiting. Right now, I could do with a beer."

He flicked a coin on the counter. The barkeep didn't smile but handed him a beer before going back to shining glasses. Mick knew he was being watched. He turned casually to look around. A couple of cowboys he didn't recognize were playing cards at one table. In the center was a pile of money.

A couple of other men were in deep conversation toward the back. They looked like they'd walked off some of the wanted posters he saw when he checked in with various sheriffs on his way back from Virginia.

Mick took his beer and sat down at an empty table. No wonder Davy was worried. This place had changed completely. He heard a door open upstairs followed by a stinging slap. A woman cried out but not one of the men in the bar moved a muscle. The door banged and still, the men sat.

Mick held the glass so tightly he thought it might snap. His instinct was to go upstairs and find out what was going on but Davy's warning rang in his ears. He knew some men hit women as a matter of course but he didn't agree with it. Still, if it was someone's wife, he couldn't intervene. The law said it was up to the husband to do as he saw fit.

He needed to get out of here. He'd find some of the men who he used to drink with when Garry was around and find out what was going on. As he sat at the table a few more men he didn't recognize came in. One went to the bar, the other made for the stairs. A couple of suggestive comments told Mick exactly what happened up there.

He drained his glass, stood up and put his hat on his head, and moved slowly toward the door. He still felt the eyes on the back of his neck, yet nobody seemed to have looked up from their cards or their conversation.

Deciding it was best to head back to the Sullivan ranch, he mounted his horse. He would talk to Grattan and the other cowboys he had often shared drinks with but not today. He would come back to town during the day and see what other changes had happened. This wasn't the Clover Springs he loved. No wonder Davy was concerned.

CHAPTER 5

Alicia helped Wilma bring the food to the table. Both had insisted Ellen rest. Father Molloy dished out some potatoes onto his plate before passing the bowl to Daniel. Katie had gone out to check the children were all playing nicely. Tilly and a few of the older orphans were looking after all the children so the adults could eat in peace.

Alicia and Mrs. Grey had decided it was better to bring up the conversation about the women after they had finished their meal. Men were much more biddable when they had a full stomach.

"That was a beautiful meal, ladies. Wilma and Mrs. H cooking for us, we were definitely eating like Kings," Father Molloy commented as he patted his stomach.

"Yes but why? What's the catch?" Aaron commented.

"Aaron Higgins, why does there have to be a catch?" Mrs. Grey asked him pretending to be annoyed.

"I know my wife and she is up to something. You got that look on your face too, Mrs. Grey. The one you get when you want us to do something." Aaron pretended to study the other ladies faces. "Katie doesn't know anything and neither does Ellen. Ma might as I still can't read her face. Wilma is as curious as I am and fit to burst."

"Mr. Aaron I got patience," Wilma protested.

"And that is the first lie of the evening."

Wilma pretended to hit Aaron with her apron while Alicia poked him in the side. She knew he was teasing but this was serious. Mrs. Grey was nervous enough and in turn, she was feeling a little anxious. How would her new friends react to her making suggestions for improving Clover Springs? She knew Wilma was on her side but hoped the other ladies wouldn't be annoyed.

"Mrs. Grey had a wonderful idea the other day. It actually works very well with something I was discussing with Wilma." Alicia took a deep breath. "I think we are all agreed Clover Springs could do with some improvements. We definitely need a bigger school and another school teacher. Aaron and I would be willing to meet the costs if you agree to proceed."

"I am?" At a poke from Alicia, Aaron nodded. "I guess I am."

Everyone smiled. "Alicia, this is wonderful news. I was so worried about how Laura would cope on her own but if we had another teacher, it would be perfect," Ellen said, nodding her head.

"It wouldn't take long to build onto the school either. We could hold a school raising instead of a barn raising. That would be fun," Katie said, her eyes shining with excitement.

"So has Mrs. Grey a new teacher picked out? Was that her idea?" Father Molloy asked.

Alicia looked to see if Mrs. Grey wanted to answer but her friend looked rather uncomfortable.

"No, not yet. We would have to advertise for the teacher. Mrs. Grey had another idea. She wants to put it before the town meeting tonight." Alicia confirmed.

"Can't you give us a little hint?"

"Aaron Higgins will you please behave. You are embarrassing Mrs. Higgins," Wilma admonished.

"Ma's used to me, Wilma."

"I think she meant me, darling." Alicia pointed at herself. The room erupted in laughter once more. Alicia had to pinch herself she was so happy. Surrounded by a loving husband, family and friends with two sons in the next room. How different it all was from when she'd first arrived. All the more reason to help Mrs. Grey now.

"We best go. The meeting will finish before we get there," Katie said as they took their leave of Ellen who was tired. She had elected to stay home telling the others to fill her in on the news tomorrow.

* * *

"Good evening everyone, thank you very much for coming to the town meeting. Before we proceed with the usual business, Mrs. Grey has asked for a couple of minutes of your time," Father Molloy greeted the townsfolk.

"What she going to lecture us about this time?"

"Mr. Staunton please take a seat. The sooner we start the quicker the meeting."

Charlie Staunton took his seat and Mrs. Grey stood up only to sit straight back down again. "Alicia, could you speak for me please."

Alicia stood. "Mrs. Grey thought, and I agree, it would be a good idea to invite some single women to come to live in Clover Springs."

At the murmurs of surprise, Alicia quickly clarified her thoughts. "You may have heard of Mr. Mercer, he's the man setting up all the railway restaurants. He employs women of good character on a minimum one year contract. In addition to their salary, he provides board and lodging. In return, they agree not to get married for the year."

"I like your idea of bringing single women to Clover Springs." Daniel yelped as Katie hit him. "I didn't mean it like that, you know you are the only woman for me."

"I am because if you so much as look at another woman Daniel Sullivan, I will kill you myself," Katie retorted.

"She loves me so much, what can I say?"

Everyone laughed at the antics knowing Daniel and Katie were as much in love as they had been when they first got married.

"Why don't you explain what you mean, Daniel?" Father Molloy suggested.

"The town is growing but we need more growth quicker. We would all benefit from more people living here," Daniel explained.

"You mean the store's profits would go through the roof. How much money do you Sullivan's need?"

"There is no need to be nasty, Mr. Staunton," Mrs. Grey chided the man who muttered grumpily under his breath.

"We don't want to turn this town into another Leadville. I want my children to grow up somewhere safe. Clover Springs was a nice place for decent folk to settle down. Or at least it was until the Red Feathers opened," Daniel continued.

The murmuring among the crowd got rather noisy making Father Molloy call for quiet.

"It's the children that made me think about this. We have so many orphans now. If we could increase the number of people living here, that should help." Mrs. Grey had finally found her voice.

"It should but I am still at a loss as to how a bunch of single ladies can help us. They can't adopt and ..." Reverend Timmons looked confused.

"They could if they get married after the initial twelve months. Most of the young ladies answering the advertisements are likely to want to marry at some point," Mrs. Grey explained.

"We all know enough about those types of advertisements," Charlie Staunton taunted.

"No, it is not like Coleman or indeed Mr. Oaks. This Mercer scheme seems to be legitimate. The ladies have to live in chaperoned quarters - I was thinking Martha Sullivan's boarding house would be perfect for that. In return for bed and lodgings, the ladies will abide by the rules which include only courting in the front parlor." Mrs. Grey took a seat once more.

"So you are going to pay them and provide food and lodgings. How would this make anyone money?" Charlie Staunton fiddled with his large mustache.

"The girls would work behind the counter in various establishments. I for one would like to see a book shop in Clover Springs, a bigger hospital, a clothes shop, a hotel, and a restaurant," Alicia answered.

"Someone could make money setting up a coffee shop near the railway. The passengers who are traveling through would be willing to spend a few dollars on some home cooked pies and proper hot coffee," Father Molloy added.

"Says a man who has spent more time than he ever wanted to traveling back and forward to Boston," Aaron shouted out.

Father Molloy smiled at the teasing.

"Having single eligible females is likely to bring a lot of menfolk to the town. There might be trouble," the sheriff added.

"But you and little Beaver can handle that can't you, Sheriff Willis?" Mrs. Grey commented.

Alicia caught the way the sheriff's chest swelled in response to the implied compliment. Mrs. Grey has an admirer. She could get her happy ever after all. She filed away that thought for another time and turned her attention back to the discussion.

"Father Molloy, what do you think of our idea?" she asked.

"In theory, I think it is wonderful. In practice, we

would need to be careful. I love Clover Springs. We already have an issue with the one saloon and house of ill repute currently here. I think if the town grows too quickly then we may end up with more problems." The priest stopped talking and looked around the room as if he could see answers on the faces before him.

Alicia couldn't help be disappointed. She'd been sure the priest would love their idea

"On the other hand, it is a wonderful charitable idea providing young girls with a safe home, good work, and a decent salary. It always amazes me how one little town can offer so much to so many. I have to put my trust in God and pray he allows us to keep the sentiment of Clover Springs while growing the population."

Alicia was sure everyone heard her breath of relief. He was in agreement.

"Going to be awful hard keeping the boys on track if they hear there are single women in town ripe for the plucking."

"Aaron Higgins," Alicia blushed. "Please mind your manners."

"Sorry, darling I forgot where I was. My apologies everyone."

"I don't agree with your language but I can appreciate your sentiment. The ranch hands will just have to realize there are rules. If they cannot abide by them then they may just find themselves out of a job. It's not like there are plenty of employment opportunities at the moment so that might be enough to keep them in line," Reverend Timmons added.

"Most of the men working for me are honest, hard-working lads who would love to find a woman and settle down. I don't expect any trouble from that quarter."

Alicia was glad to hear Davy stick up for his men.

"Not all men are so well behaved, Mr. Sullivan." Mrs. Grey's pointed glance in Charlie Staunton's direction didn't go unnoticed.

"So how do we find these girls?" Alicia asked in the hope of diffusing any potential row.

"I am sure Nellie will help us. She is bound to know people whose families need work," Katie said before explaining to Alicia who Nellie was. "Nellie was the cook in our Uncle's house when we first came to Boston. She looked after Ellen and me."

"But ain't she working for Mrs. Gantley the mail-order bride lady?" Wilma said.

"Yes she is but it will be all right. Not everyone who arrives at Mrs. Gantley's house is suitable to be a mail-order bride. Some are just so desperate for a job and security, they are willing to get married. I am sure Mrs. Gantley will help us too. She will have connections with rich people who employ servants. Many Irish and English people come to America by following family members."

"Father Molloy, do you have any ideas?" Alicia asked for fear their project would lose his backing.

"Indeed I do. Lots of Irish girls have been in service back in Ireland and often come to Boston with wonderful references. But as you know yourselves there are more servants than there are jobs in Boston at the moment."

"These are the girls the likes of Coleman will prey on. They are in a new country, probably worried sick about their future and will jump at any chance to earn what they think is a decent living," Alicia commented.

"That's true and many a young girl has got caught by groups like Coleman's and your friend, Mr. Venebles."

Alicia shuddered at the mention of her ex-fiancé. "He most certainly isn't my friend. I hope he rots in jail."

"So do you think this will work, Father?" Katie asked.

"Well Katie, I certainly think it's worth a try don't you?"

CHAPTER 6

Erin twisted and turned, trying to find a comfortable position. She was heartily sick of sitting on a train and wished more than once she had put Mam's parcel in the post. Her mam would never have known any different and she wouldn't be sitting here on a train headed to goodness knows where.

She wasn't looking forward to meeting a Catholic priest. Her mam's last wish before she got on the boat back to Ireland was for Erin to follow her Catholic upbringing. It's not just about religion, Alannah, it's about being part of a large family.

Erin had hugged her mam tightly. She only ever called them Alannah when she was very upset, falling into the Gaelic endearment easily. Erin had hugged her two younger brothers and her sister as they made their way back to Ireland. Her mam's brother had promised them a home. Mam couldn't stay in New York, not after what had happened to her husband.

Things were better in Ireland, the famine was a thing of the past. The economy had picked up a lot too, probably due in part to the amount of money being sent home by the Irish in America. Da had always wanted to go "home" as he called it despite being born in New York. Erin guessed this was her mam's way of feeling closer to him. She had tried to convince Erin to go with them. The chances of becoming a doctor in America were slim but there were none in Ireland. Over there a woman's place was very firmly in the home. Erin shuddered. She couldn't imagine anything worse than being stuck at home minding children, cooking and washing while her husband worked all the hours God sent to keep a roof over their heads.

* * *

SHE WATCHED out the window as the train puffed into Clover Springs. She was looking forward to a good wash and a comfortable night's sleep. Thankfully she was wearing a traveling cloak so it took the brunt of the ashes and cinders flying around. She would be glad to get rid of it, it was so ugly and patched in so many places it was a wonder it stuck together. But it served its purpose as Mam would have said. She smiled as the conductor helped her off the train.

"I hope you enjoy your stay here, miss, although I doubt you will stay unmarried for a whole year."

Erin shuck her head at his strange comment. He had made similar ones on the train. She supposed he saw so many passengers he had got her mixed up with someone else. A new mail-order bride on her way to meet her husband perhaps. The male doctors she had worked with back in New York, had found it hilarious someone would travel across the country to marry a man they hadn't met. But it was different for them. They had choices. Most of the women in the adverts in the Newspapers were obviously desperate.

"Well looks like Mrs. Grey's idea is off to a good start, would you say Mick?"

Erin spun around to stare coldly as two cowboys stood staring at her. The man she assumed was Mick had the decency to look away, embarrassed to be caught staring. The other man simply stared back even when she tried imitating her mother's steely look.

"Looks a mite bad-tempered to me but guess that could be the traveling. Maybe I should offer to carry her bag and see if that sweetens her up some." The cowboy winked at Erin.

"I would suggest you mind your manners or

perhaps go and learn some. I can look after my own bags, thank you very much." She turned on her heel and walked off in the direction of a hut. She hoped there was a train official on duty. Thankfully, an older man stood behind the counter. "Please sir, could you watch my luggage until I return with some transport?"

"Where are you traveling to, miss?"

"I am looking for a boarding house."

"Ah, you are one of the girls. Funny I thought you would be younger." The man spat some tobacco out the side of his mouth. Erin stared in horror at the brown juice making its way down his bushy beard. She didn't know what shocked her more, the fact he seemed to be expecting her or the fact he'd called her old. Twenty-six she may be but old? What sort of town was this anyway?

"Thank you," she muttered as politely as she could. It wouldn't do to annoy the man looking after her belongings.

"Quinn, can ya show this lady to the boarding house please. I got to mind her bags," the bearded man shouted.

"Any excuse for you to sit while others do your bidding Matthews," the man called back although he nodded to Erin as he removed his hat. "Names Mick Quinn. If you come with me ma'am, I will show you to the Sullivan boarding house. Mrs. Sullivan is expecting you."

* * *

MICK COULDN'T BELIEVE his luck. Matthews had asked him to show the new girl to the boarding house. She wasn't bad looking if she smiled. She'd taken offense really easy though but then Grattan wasn't known for his tact. He spent way too much time around animals to remember how to speak to a lady. Maybe she was embarrassed they all knew why she was in Clover Springs.

"Mrs. Sullivan, she runs the boarding house, is a very nice lady. She'll look out for you."

Erin looked at him quickly before looking away. He tried again.

"So what's your name? You know mine," he said smiling.

"Erin Brennan."

"So Miss Brennan, where are you from?"

"New York."

Well, it was a start, she'd answered his question. Maybe she didn't like to talk. He couldn't imagine that. All the ladies he had met loved talking. Mary, Laura and Mrs. H never stopped talking from what he saw at the ranch.

"What made you decide to come to Clover Springs?" Sort of a stupid question to ask when you know the answer. All the ladies coming to stay with Mrs. Sullivan wanted to get married didn't they?

Mick found himself walking alone. He turned to see the lady standing on the path behind him. What was wrong with her? He walked back.

"What you standing here for? The boarding house is up there a bit."

"I am trying to work out why everyone thinks my business is theirs. Does nothing ever happen in this town? Are you so short of people to speak to, you subject complete strangers to an interrogation?"

Gee, she was madder than a cornered beast. "Listen, lady, don't get uppity with me. I was just making conversation. I won't say another word."

"Thank you." She walked off leaving him no option but to follow her. He had offered to carry her carpet bag but she clung to it closely. He admired the way her skirts swished showing a tantalizing view of shapely ankles before he realized she had taken the wrong turn. At this rate, she would be in the Red Feathers or the saloon next door. Mrs. Sullivan would kill him if that happened closely followed by Mrs. Grey. He called out to her but she didn't seem to hear him. Either that or she was ignoring him deliberately. He was tempted to let her keep walking to see what she would make of the saloon.

Her step didn't falter. Even when a scantily clad Lily said hi to her. In fact, he could swear the lady returned the greeting and spoke a few words to the girl. Lily seemed stunned, she was probably really surprised to find a respectable lady speaking to her. Lily replied and then the lady kept on walking. Was she a fake? Maybe he should warn someone the first lady to respond to their advert for virtuous young ladies didn't seem to mind talking to saloon girls.

* * *

ERIN KEPT WALKING WONDERING how far the boarding house could be. The girl she had asked said it was a couple of houses down on the right. Would it have a sign outside? Maybe the cowboy would catch up with her in time. She didn't fancy arriving at the wrong door.

A loud bang followed by a horrific wailing scream pierced the air. "That came from the direction of the mill," Mick said. "Someone go fetch Doc and Mrs. Grey."

"Please show me where the mill is," Erin said.

"Not now, Ma'am. Wouldn't be right to bring a lady."

“I am not a lady. I am a doctor and judging by the sounds of those screams, my skills are needed." Erin moved quickly in the direction of the screams, leaving Mick standing behind her with his mouth open

A doctor? He’d thought she was one of the new girls Mrs. Grey was bringing to Clover Springs. Mick ran after Erin. Grabbing her elbow he half pulled her along until they reached the mill. The sight was not pleasant.

"Pa was trying to fix the blade but somehow it turned on. I tried to turn it off but... it took a few seconds,” a young boy said, his face chalk white save for the splatters of blood.

"Get the child out of here. Make sure he gets a warm drink and someone put a blanket around him after they wash him." Erin was examining the adult while issuing instructions. Nobody moved. "Don’t just stand around gaping at me. I am a doctor. Do what I say."

Mick recognized Mrs. Larkin who was a mother of ten. She moved forward putting her arm around the young lad’s shoulders. "Come with me Max, we will get you cleaned up while the doc looks after your pa."

"I don’t want to leave him. He needs me,” Max whimpered.

"Your ma will need you too. I think Wilma may have been making cookies. Let's go find out."

Mrs. Larkin led the child away. Erin was kneeling down beside Mr. Hofmeister.

"Where's Doc?" Daniel Sullivan's white face showed his panic.

"He's out at the Rankin place. Won't be back for hours. Mrs. Grey is following behind. Mrs. Shipley stayed at the clinic," someone answered.

"Where is the clinic?" Erin asked

"A couple of blocks down the street. We will have to carry him."

The men moved forward but Erin stopped them. "Don't touch him."

"Lady, if we don't get him to the clinic he will die."

"If you move him, he will bleed to death in seconds." Erin opened Mr. Hofmeister's shirt and appeared to listen to his breathing. "Mr. Hofmeister, can you hear me? We are going to do everything to help you. Please stay calm. I am going to give you something for the pain."

Mr. Hofmeister didn't reply. Erin reached into her bag.

"Thank God you are here Mrs. Grey. This young lady won't let us move Hans. She says we will kill him."

"She's right." Mrs. Grey assessed the scene quickly. "I am a nurse. What can I do?"

Erin sent her a grateful look.

"Thankfully he missed the main artery but there is

a lot of blood. I need clean cloths and water to see where most of the bleeding is coming from. I could do with someone mechanical too. I have to remove the blades."

Mrs. Grey sent some of the women off to get bowls of water. She had brought the cloths with her. She stripped them into smaller pieces to soak up as much of the blood as she could.

"Do you have any chloroform in the clinic?" Erin asked.

Mrs. Grey nodded.

"I think it would be kinder to put Hans asleep while we remove the blade," Erin explained.

"The risks..."

"Are huge either way," Erin interrupted in a strained tone.

Mrs. Grey stood again. "Mick, go to the clinic and ask Mrs. Shipley for the bottle of chloroform. Be careful with it."

"Yes, ma'am".

CHAPTER 7

Erin wiped her head with her sleeve as the perspiration threatened to drip into her eyes. She squeezed her eyes shut quickly trying to remember every bit of the lectures on amputation. She couldn't save the man's arm. He would die if she didn't take the arm off. If they were in the hospital, she would feel fairly confident. She had assisted at enough amputations but operate out here in the open? She wasn't sure she was up to that. Especially with all these people around.

The man, Quinn wasn't it, returned with the chloroform. Mrs. Grey administered it to the patient who, at least now, was out of pain.

"The arm will have to come off," Mrs. Grey said quietly.

Erin looked up, straight into the older woman's

eyes.

"Yes, but ..."

"You have never performed such a procedure?" Mrs. Grey asked.

"Not that exactly. I have assisted at a number of them but in a hospital with a proper bed and the right equipment. Not here in public."

"Well, we got to do the best we can. Otherwise, he will die."

At Erin's look, Mrs. Grey gave her a quick pat on the hand. "If you don't do anything he will die. If you try, he may live. Which choice do you think he would make?"

Erin nodded while steeling herself to carry out the operation. She watched Mrs. Grey get ready as she washed her hands in one of the many bowls of hot water.

"You have done this before haven't you?" Erin asked.

"Yes, back in the war. Not a skill I hoped to have to use again, it has to be said." Mrs. Grey looked grim.

Erin hoped her hands wouldn't start trembling. She wished the people would go away but, if anything, they had moved closer - probably wanted a better view.

She looked around in despair, her glance caught the intense gaze of the man they called Quinn.

CHAPTER 8

"Right people, give the doc room. Mrs. Grey won't be able to breathe if you don't move back. Go on now, I'm sure you all have things to be doing." Mick turned to a boy standing closest to him. "Bertram Shaw make yourself useful and go get the reverend."

"Is he going to die?" The hope glistening in young Shaw's eyes made Mick look away.

"I hope not young man, now get out of here."

The boy ran off up the road, no doubt eager to share with his friends what was Wilma to bake at the mill.

You could have heard a pin drop on the street, it was so quiet. Well, apart from the noise of the saw. Mick, who prided himself on his steady stomach, had to walk away. He couldn't bear the image the noise was created in his head. It brought back awful memories of the Yankee hospital he'd been in. How could a young woman do something like that? She must have a cast iron stomach.

He saw Mrs. Grey quickly wrap something up in a blanket. Then she got to her feet. "Mick, can you and a couple of the other men fetch a wagon so we can move Mr. Hofmeister to the clinic, please. Perhaps you could find someone to clean up here before his wife sees it?"

"Yes, ma'am." Mick rounded up a couple of the boys and together they helped carry the unconscious man into the wagon. Mick offered his hand to the Doctor to help her climb into the back. She smiled - the smile of a professional acknowledging the help but it set the hairs on the back of Mick's neck to rise. He smiled back but it was too late, she was concentrating fully on her patient once more.

They made their way to the clinic very slowly. Mrs. Grey riding up front with Mick while the doc sat with Hofmeister.

"Will he make it?" Mick asked Mrs. Grey.

Mrs. Grey looked back at the patient before answering. "Not sure but if Hans does, you will have the doctor to thank."

Somehow Mick didn't think the doctor would take kindly to his thanks. Not when he'd mistaken her for a husband seeker.

CHAPTER 9

Erin nursed the patient through the night and next morning only taking breaks when Mrs. Grey insisted. She soon learned nobody said no to Mrs. Grey. The Clover Springs doctor didn't come back - someone said it wasn't unusual for the trip to take a few days. She wished he was here. She would have welcomed a second opinion. Mr. Hofmeister seemed to be doing all right but there was something about his condition making her wary.

"You aren't totally happy with him, are you?" Mrs. Grey asked her quietly.

"How did you know?"

"I take it you don't make a habit of frowning at your patients."

Erin rubbed her face. "I am not sure what it is. He seems to be recovering but..."

"You trust your instinct. It's what differentiates good doctors. I will stay here with you so you can rest more."

Mrs. Grey insisted Erin went for a nap in the other examination room. She promised to call her if anything changed. It didn't but still, Erin couldn't rest easy.

* * *

The next afternoon, Mr. Hofmeister was well enough to see his wife and son. They had been waiting in the clinic since the accident. Erin was worried about Mrs. Hofmeister as she was heavily pregnant but the lady insisted she wanted to be near her husband. Mrs. Grey arranged for them to sleep upstairs at the clinic.

Mr. Hofmeister was very thankful to Erin and Mrs. Grey for saving his life. He didn't seem to realize his arm was gone. He kept talking about how good it would be to get out of the hospital and back to work. He had a lot of big orders on his books and he couldn't afford to lose the customers. There was another mill in the next town so his customers had an alternative.

Erin couldn't understand a word of German but she saw how Mrs. Hofmeister reassured her husband. The lady bravely pushed aside her own concerns, smiling brightly at her husband telling him all would be well. It was only when her gaze met Erin's, that Erin saw the unmasked fear for a couple of seconds. It was quickly replaced by a look of steely determination. Erin sighed. These two people obviously loved each other deeply.

CHAPTER 10

Mrs. Grey told Erin, she had arranged for her belongings to be collected from the station and moved to the boarding house. She persuaded Erin to go and have a bath and get changed. One of the boys from the orphanage showed her the way. He was tickled pink when she gave him a coin for his trouble. The front door was open so she went inside hoping to have a hot bath. Mrs. Sullivan came out of the drawing room just as she closed the front door.

"Miss Brennan I have been hearing so much about you. Congratulations on saving Mr. Hofmeister. He hasn't lived here long. He is a lovely man and his wife is such a dear. She is due soon too."

Erin didn't say anything but let Mrs. Sullivan chatter on. She was so tired she couldn't think of a response. Plus she couldn't tell the lady it was too early to feel such confidence.

"Mrs. Sullivan, I wondered if I could have a bath."

"Yes of course dear. Mick Quinn dropped off your bags earlier and Mrs. Grey sent one of the boys ahead to tell us you were coming back for a break. You will find everything you need in your room."

"Mrs. Grey is so nice to me," Erin commented and wondered at the look Mrs. Sullivan gave her but she didn't waste time worrying about it. She wanted a bath and then bed.

Finally feeling clean, she put on a fresh nightdress and got into bed. As soon as her head hit the pillow her mind woke up. She couldn't sleep for thoughts of what she could have done, should have done, might have done. After a couple of hours tossing and turning she gave up, got dressed and made her way downstairs. She followed some delicious smells finding herself in the kitchen where Mrs. Sullivan was stirring something on the stove.

"Up already? I thought you might sleep for a few hours. Mrs. Grey will be cross."

"Mrs. Sullivan, why was there a rock in my bed?"

"To warm it up for you love. Haven't you heard of that before?"

Erin shook her head. She didn't want to tell the

lovely woman she'd been used to the luxury of indoor plumbing and heating back in New York.

"We call it the spinster's friend. No offense meant, only it warms up your legs."

The rock did a good job. She smiled at the name. If only they knew.

"So why didn't you sleep?" Mrs. Sullivan asked, her face a mask of concern.

"I couldn't relax."

"Is there something wrong with the bed? Do you not feel comfortable?"

"No, it's not that at all," Erin said hastily. "It was more my thoughts. I was thinking about what happened and..." Her voice drained away

"Doc Brennan if you weren't here, Hans would have died. By acting as you did, you gave him a chance. Will he live? That's in God's hands now. You have done your best."

"But you weren't even there. Were you?" Erin asked.

"No, but Mrs. Grey doesn't give out praise lightly. According to her, you did a fine job."

Erin sat down at the table forgetting to ask if she could. Mrs. Sullivan placed a hot cup of coffee and some oat and raisin cookies in front of her.

"Your parents must be very proud of you. To have a daughter a doctor."

"Mam was. Da died years back before I finished school."

"Sorry to hear that. So what brings you to Clover Springs?"

"Husband hunting if the gossip is anything to go by." Erin smiled in response to the look on Mrs. Sullivan's face. "I am teasing Mrs. Sullivan. I think the men at the station mistook me for somebody else."

"Yes, I believe they did. We weren't expecting a doctor."

"Especially a lady one," Erin remarked but continued, " although I have to say, I haven't seen any real resistance to the idea of a lady doctor."

"You will."

Erin laughed. "You don't beat about the bush, Mrs. Sullivan."

"No point dear. In this life, some men are still trying to get around to the idea that women have a working brain. You just have to get on with it. But I didn't know we had advertised for a doctor. Is our town doc retiring and didn't tell anyone?"

"Not that I know of. My visit here is only temporary. I have to give something to someone and then I will be moving on. I have some job interviews lined up in Denver."

"Job interviews," Mrs. Sullivan repeated, "So you haven't secured employment as such."

“Not yet, no." Erin wasn’t about to admit her chances of securing employment were rather low.

"What's the attraction in Denver?" Mrs. Sullivan asked after a couple of minutes of silence had passed comfortably.

"Attraction? Well none really. I need a job and they have a lot of hospitals and medical facilities."

'What about your mam? Didn’t she want you to stay close to where she lives? I hate my Elizabeth lives miles outside town. If I get to see her once a month, I am lucky."

"Mam went back to Ireland. She said it was Daddy's wish and she wanted to fulfill it. I don’t think she could bear living here without him."

"I never thought I would see the day when people were leaving America to go back home,” Mrs. Sullivan said, a look of yearning on her face. “Things seem to have improved back there a lot."

"Maybe. I think in Mam's case, it wouldn’t really matter. She has enough to live on and her brother, who owns a large farm, has offered her a home. I miss them but it’s nice to see them out of the slums of New York." Erin stirred her tea wondering what her mam was up to right this minute.

"I heard it's bad there. In New York.”

"It's worse than you could ever imagine, Mrs. Sullivan. All those people living on top of one another.

There are so many people arriving every day from different countries, seeking the pavements made out of gold. Often they find they are worse off than they were back in their own countries. At least there they could speak the language and knew the customs. A lot of fights break out over misunderstandings and cultural differences."

CHAPTER 11

Mick rode back into town, his mind filling with images. They wouldn't go away not until he had drunk enough whiskey. He thought of young Max. He'd been his age when he'd left home, forced to fight in a war he didn't agree with. His pa had died and his regiment needed new men. Times were different then. If Hans died, nobody would send his child off to war.

Mick tied his horse to the hitching rail. Pushing open the doors of the saloon he was hit by the smell of sawdust. Dickinson must have put fresh down to cover up the old smells. Unfortunately, the stale tobacco and cheap perfume weren't enough to cover the other odors. Not looking left or right he strode up to the bar.

The barkeep poured him a shot of whiskey.

"Leave the bottle," Mick said. The barkeep gave him a look but didn't say anything. He picked up a cloth and started polishing glasses. Mick hit the shot back in one, poured another and another, but it wasn't working. It seemed with every glass the images in his mind became clearer. He sensed someone at his elbow.

Surprised he found himself looking into the face of a young woman. Women weren't allowed into the saloon at least they weren't in Gary's day.

"My name's Mollie. You look like you need some company stranger." Mollie smiled but the smile didn't reach her eyes. Under all the gaudy clothes and makeup, she was only a kid. How did she end up in a place like this?

"Go away, Mollie."

The smile fell from her face. She sidled closer. "Aw don't be like that Mick. You're really good looking."

"You say that to all the boys."

"Sure I do, but I only mean it when I say it to you."

For a second Mick was tempted to take her upstairs but the thought disappeared as soon as it came.

"Mick, are you coming or not?" Mollie was tugging on his arm, her eyes filled with terror. He looked in the mirror to see what was causing that. Dickinson or Dickie as he liked to be called, stood at the bottom of the stairs, he seemed to be smiling but as usual, he had the cold calculating look in his eyes.

"Please Mick, I'll do anything you want. But don't say no." Although she spoke very softly he couldn't miss the note of desperation in her voice.

Grabbing the bottle with his other hand, Mick allowed Mollie to lead him upstairs. He ignored the whistles from Trigger and the other Sullivan ranch hands. They must have followed him into town. He did notice the exchange between Mollie and Dickie. Mollie looked like an abused dog he had adopted years ago. Terrified her owner would beat her yet begging for acknowledgment.

THEY GOT to Mollie's room or at least the room she pretended was hers. Mick very much doubted Dickie kept his girls in this much luxury. She sat on the bed, waiting he guessed for him to ask for something.

"Mollie, why do you work here?"

Mollie looked astonished to be asked. A flush spread over her neck and upwards to her face.

"Why? What's it got to do with you?"

Mick walked over to the chair by the bed. He sat down, putting his feet up on the bed. He threw a few coins on the cover. Mollie picked them up greedily.

"I was just curious. You seem so young."

“I ain’t never been young,” Mollie said before straightening her shoulders. "I am plenty old enough."

"Ain't you ever wanted to do something else?” he probed.

The hard mask slipped once more and he saw she was even younger than he had first thought.

"I wanted to be a teacher once. You know like Miss Ellen from the orphanage. I was good at school. I know you probably think that’s funny."

“I ain’t laughing.”

Mollie looked at him as if to check he wasn’t making fun of her. Satisfied he was genuine, she continued with a little more enthusiasm. "I was good. I got an apple from the teacher more than once. But then Ma died and Pa, well he... he wasn’t the same after Ma went. He started drinking. One drink became a bottle and ... "

Mick knew the rest of the story without hearing it. It was a similar one to the one he had heard over and over searching for his sisters.

"So are you, you know?” Mollie gestured toward the bed. She looked extremely uncomfortable, or was she nervous?

"Why are you frightened?" he asked, feeling a little stupid as soon as the words were out of his mouth.

"I'm not afraid of anything." Mollie’s defensive tone would have made him smile as she sounded like a child caught doing something wrong. But for the fact, they were sitting in a bedroom over a saloon.

"Easy Mollie, I paid for the time. Nobody but you and I are going to know what happens in here."

"You mean you just going to sit there."

"Yup."

"The whole time?" she looked like she wanted to believe him but couldn't.

"Yup."

Mollie eyed him curiously. He watched as the curiosity was replaced by doubt. "Do you not like girls?" She edged toward the door.

He laughed. "I like girls just fine. I'm tired and I suspect you are too. I thought we could just spend a while relaxing, maybe chat a bit."

"Chat? You mean you want to talk to me? Ain't you got any friends?" Mollie moved back toward the bed, picking at the bedspread.

Mick pondered the question. Had he any friends? Davy was a good boss but were they friends? Cookie, he was his friend. He was more than a friend, he was like family. But otherwise, there was no one.

"I guess not. Do you?"

Mollie shrugged. "The girls here are nice. I guess."

"What about home? Anyone left there?"

The shutters came down immediately. "Nope."

She was lying but Mick wasn't about to ask why.

"About Dickie. Does he beat you?"

Mollie stared at some point above his head. "I don't want to say nothing about Dickie."

"All right. You look tired, why don't you have a nap?"

"Go to sleep. On this bed?" Mollie looked at the bed with longing in her eyes.

"Yes, get into bed and go asleep. I will wake you in time, don't worry."

"But Dickie," she hesitated.

"He would expect the bed to be used."

Mollie flushed before turning her back to him and taking off her dress. He guessed she didn't want it crumpled. He closed his eyes as she slid under the covers. She was asleep seconds after her head hit the pillow. He stared at her face, so much younger looking now. He wanted to pull the covers around her and take her away from here. But there was nowhere for them to go.

You're going soft Mick Quinn. He pushed his hat down over his eyes and settled back for a nap.

A while later, loud knocking woke him. He scrambled to the door, opening it a fraction.

"Your time is up, fella," Dickie stood on the doorstep, one foot near the door so Mick couldn't close it.

"How much for the night?" he asked.

"Three dollars."

Mick flinched, he knew the rate wasn't that high but he paid it anyway. He could look out for Mollie for one night. He handed over three dollars fifty cents. "Give the barkeep the rest. I owe him for some whiskey. Don't disturb us again."

He caught the dirty grin on Dickie's face but shut the door. He didn't want to antagonize anyone. Not now. He had to come up with a plan. Now he had met Mollie he had to find a way to get her out of here.

* * *

DAWN BROKE JUST as he woke Mollie. She sat up with a start clutching the bedclothes to her.

"I stayed here all night?"

"It's all right. I paid Dickie. He's happy. I have to go now but I will be back again. If you ever need anything, Mollie, you send someone for me."

He saw by her face she wouldn't. She didn't trust anyone. He couldn't blame her.

"I mean it, Molly."

"I don't know anything about you. I just heard the barkeep call you Mick one night."

"Why did you pick me last night then?"

"You looked decent." Her soft voice made him pause. He glanced in the mirror at his old clothes, his bearded face and too long hair. Decent wasn't a word that came to mind.

"I work out on the Sullivan ranch. If you can't find me go to Wilma. She's at the orphanage," Mick said gruffly, trying to hide his emotions.

Mollies face brightened. "I like Wilma. She's kind to me. She says hello when she's passin'."

"Well, go to Wilma. Promise?"

A long silence lingered. Mick tried not to show his impatience but if he didn't get moving fast, he would be late to the ranch. He didn't mind the ribbing from the hands, but he didn't want to be on Davy's bad side.

"I will."

On impulse, Mick leaned forward. He stopped as she shrunk back from him.

"Mollie, I ain't ever hit no woman and I ain't about to start now. You take care, you hear." He kissed her lightly on the forehead before pushing down his hat. Closing the door behind him, he hoped he wouldn't meet Dickie on the stairs. That was one man who he wouldn't mind feeling the full force of his fist.

CHAPTER 12

Erin knew the minute she walked into the clinic, there as something wrong. The smell told her. She washed her hands hurriedly before joining Mrs. Grey at Hans' bedside. The look the other woman gave her confirmed her suspicions.

"Gangrene?"

"Certainly smells like it and I thought he was getting so much better," Mrs. Grey's spoke in a whisper.

"We will have to operate again."

"But how? You already cut close to the shoulder." Mrs. Grey seemed to realize what she had said. "Sorry doctor I shouldn't have questioned you."

"No, you are quite right. It will be difficult and I am not sure he will survive the operation. Even if he does, his chances of survival are grim. I have never seen a patient recover after losing so much blood. The operation took too long."

"You did the best you could. You don't go thinking anything else," Mrs. Grey insisted.

"Where's the doctor, I wouldn't mind his opinion?" Erin asked, wishing she was back in the New York hospital.

"You missed him although he said he was looking forward to meeting you. He was called out earlier but he had already suggested if it was his patient he wouldn't operate again. No point in raising false hope he said." Mrs. Grey looked at the patient, her expression grave.

Erin wavered. She could see the doctor's point but then there was Mrs. Hofmeister and their young boy, Max. What would they do without a husband and a father?

"Excuse me, Doctor, can I speak to you please?"

Erin looked up to find herself staring at Mrs. Hofmeister. She hadn't realized the woman was in the room. She wouldn't have spoken so plainly if she had.

"I am glad I hear you speak frankly. My Hans would not want to be cripple. He did not come all this way to be a burden. Please, not cut him again. But can you give him something so he is not in pain?"

Erin nodded, she had a frog in her throat and couldn't speak. She caught Mrs. Grey brush a tear from her face too. The bravery of the young foreign woman was astonishing. She loved her husband so much. It was written all over her face.

"Mrs. Hofmeister, I will do everything I can to make sure he is comfortable," Erin promised.

"Ja. We will let him think he is better. I must get my son ready for school. It is best he is not here now."

Erin couldn't agree more. A hospital bed was no place for a child. Nobody needed to see their pa die. She'd had no choice but ...

* * *

Mrs. Hofmeister stayed by her husband's side for the next thirty- six hours. In lucid moments, Hans spoke about his mill and how much money he had waiting in orders. He became agitated at one point and Mrs. Grey had to find help to hold him down. One of the men who rushed to help was the man who had walked her from the train to the boarding house. He seemed very uncomfortable - natural given the man was dying. But it was more than that. He kept looking at Mrs. Hofmeister. Maybe he wants to marry her. Mrs. Sullivan said there was a severe shortage of women but, surely, he could wait for her husband to get a decent burial.

Mr. Hofmeister finally lost his battle in the early hours of the following morning. He woke for a few minutes almost as if he wanted to say goodbye. Erin had to leave the room rather than listen to him profess his love for his wife and her to him. She crept back in as Mrs. Hofmeister dissolved into tears. It had taken all her strength to keep brave for her husband and now he was gone, she could freely express her emotions. After an hour, Erin gave her a mild sedative afraid she would damage herself in the grieving process. While Mrs. Hofmeister slept, Erin helped Mrs. Grey lay out and prepare Mr. Hofmeister's body.

"You should go home and rest doctor."

"You should too Mrs. Grey. In fact, as the doctor, I order you to."

"Nobody orders me anywhere dear," the older woman protested mildly.

"And that's a fact you best get used to," a male voice added.

Erin jumped, she hadn't noticed the older man come in. She guessed he was the town doctor.

"Now why don't both of you go home and let me take over from here. Dr. Brennan, I know what it is like to lose a patient but in this case, you did everything you could." He smiled at her, his kindness making his eyes gleam.

"Thank you, Doctor." Erin didn't believe him but none of that mattered now. The patient was dead, the bereaved family would return to their life such as it was now. It always amazed her how life went on no matter what horrible events one had to deal with.

CHAPTER 13

Erin walked back to the boarding house, taking a more scenic route past the mill. She was amazed to see it working with a group of men around it. The Cowboy as she had taken to calling him seemed to be in the center of things.

"Morning, Doc."

The men turned to stare at her. Embarrassed at being caught in public so disheveled she hurried along up the street barely returning their greeting. She arrived in the door just as Martha Sullivan walked into the kitchen.

Horrified, she felt tears running down her face.

“Come here to me Alannah. There you let those tears out. There was nothing you could have done. Do you hear me? You did the best you could.” Martha soothed her just like her mam would have.

Erin cried and cried until finally her tears were spent. She dried her eyes with her soaking handkerchief.

"I am going to make you a proper cup of tea. Nothing better to take the mind off bad things."

Erin smiled through a fresh set of tears. Her mam always did the same. Said nothing cured anything better than a cup of tea. If only it were true.

"What are the men doing at the mill? Has someone taken over already?"

"No, that's the town helping one of their own. Mick, he works out on Davy's ranch, got a few men together and they agreed to fulfill the orders Hans had. At least Mrs. Hofmeister and young Max will have some money to keep them going. They should get a better price for the mill too if they sell it as a thriving business."

Erin could have cried all over again. He had been trying to help all along and she had misjudged him. She still hadn't learned anything about a man's character, had she?

Mrs. Sullivan placed the cup of tea in front of Erin with a plateful of cookies.

"Bit early I know but nothing better to cure the heart than a little bit of sugar."

Erin bit into a cookie, smiling at her hostess.

Curiosity finally got the better of her and she asked, “How well do you know him?”

“Who Mick? Not well at all really. He used to work out at Davy's place - he's my son who now owns the ranch his pa set up. My Davy is a fine man but when his wife, Mary, first arrived as a mail order bride, he had a bit of a jealous streak. Mick helped Mary to buy a present for Davy, but Davy got the wrong idea. There wasn't a fight as much as the men were uncomfortable with the atmosphere. Mick cleared off soon afterward.” Mrs. Sullivan took a sip of tea before continuing. “Then he came back a couple of years ago. He comes and goes doing odd jobs here and there. Davy trusts him and that says a lot."

"So he wasn’t making eyes at Mrs. Sullivan?"

"Not at all dear, that was all in Davy's imagination. Mary wouldn’t look at another man, she fell head over heels for my son soon after they got married.”

Erin couldn’t imagine how someone could marry a stranger never mind fall in love with them after the ceremony.

"Why are you asking? Have you your eye on Mick?”

Erin blushed scarlet even though she knew Mrs. Sullivan was teasing.

"He seemed very keen on helping Mrs. Hofmeister.”

"Mick's like that especially if there is a child around. Rumor has it part of the reason he goes away so much is he is looking for his own child. I don't stand for gossip. The man has his own reasons for living a life on the road but when he is in Clover Springs, he always does his best for the widows and their children."

Erin felt bad. She had decided he was acting like a cad when it seemed his motives were purely charitable. "I guess being bought up in New York, I have a suspicious mind."

Mrs. Sullivan stared at her for a couple of seconds. "I'd say you have seen more horrors than most. I read the papers. I know from speaking to Wilma and Laura, you haven't met them yet, the horrible things happening in our big cities. The sheer numbers of people living in such a small area are bound to bring the bad as well as the good. But for what it's worth, Mick seems to be one of the good guys."

"He limps slightly. Doesn't it affect his job as a ranch hand?" Erin asked.

"That's an old war wound. Doesn't seem to affect his riding. Gets worse when he has been working too hard or so Cookie says."

"Did he fight in the Indian wars?"

"I don't know but the wound I was speaking of happened at Atlanta."

"You mean in the Civil War?" Erin knew she sounded shocked. "But he doesn't look old enough."

"He wasn't. Cookie says he was about twelve or thirteen although he told the officers he was older. They didn't care at that point. The Confederates were so desperate for men."

"He fought for the South?"

"Erin, take some advice from an older woman. There is never anything black or white with war. I have never seen Mick treat anyone with disrespect. He is a firm favorite of Wilma's and of Little Beaver."

Erin took the hint but she couldn't help feeling disappointed. Her father had fought in the Union Army. He and Mick could have been shooting at one another. Him and a thousand others. Why are you thinking about Mick all the time?

She decided to change the subject.

"What will happen to Mrs. Hofmeister? I haven't been here long but there doesn't seem to be many German families in town."

"No there isn't. Not because they aren't welcome, I guess some would see Clover Springs as being predominantly Irish. I am sure Mrs. Shaw feels that way."

"Who?" Erin didn't think she had met a Mrs. Shaw.

"You haven't met her yet. I will let you make your

own mind up about her. Now I best get on with my day. What are you up to? Will you go to bed to rest?"

"I thought I would call on Mrs. Hofmeister to check on her. She is heavily pregnant."

"Oh yes, you asked me about her. I heard she plans to go to stay with relatives in Kansas."

"She can't travel all that way now. She will have to wait until the baby comes," Erin protested.

Mrs. Sullivan looked upset. "Financially that option may not be available. I would offer to let her stay here but I have already promised the six rooms to Father Molloy and Mrs. Grey."

"As her doctor, I won't let her travel. The shock of her husband's death is enough to make her go into labor early. She needs watching."

Mrs. Sullivan laughed. "You remind me of Katie, my daughter-in-law. She works in the store. When she gets an idea in her head, she has to make it happen. You two will get on well."

Erin hoped so. She missed her mam more than she was willing to let on. Not just because she was her mother but because she was also a good friend. Her mam! She hadn't delivered the package to Father Molloy.

"I forgot I have to see Father Molloy. Can you point me towards his house please?"

Mrs. Sullivan gave her directions to the Timmons house where Father Molloy was staying. Erin washed her face and hands and redid her hair. Then taking a deep breath and the gift she headed outside to find Father Molloy.

CHAPTER 14

She knocked on the door and a smiling lady, introducing herself as Mrs. Timmons ushered her in to see Father Molloy. She felt uncomfortable as he looked busy.

"Father Molloy, do you have a minute please?"

"Good morning, come in and find a seat. As you can see I am in a bit of muddle. I wrote my sermon for church and now I can't find it."

Erin looked around the room. There were books everywhere on every conceivable surface including the seat he had indicated. She picked them up and took a seat. Not having anywhere to put them, she left them on her knee.

"You are the new doctor in town, aren't you?"

"News spreads quickly."

"You did a great job for Hans, God rest his soul. I

did call by the clinic to introduce myself but Mrs. Grey had sent you home for a rest. Very sensible lady is Mrs. Grey."

Very formidable too but Erin wasn't about to comment.

"What can I do for you, Doc Brennan?"

"I wanted to thank you. Mam, Mairead Brennan I mean, gave me this to give you." She handed him the gift her mother had left with her. "She said it was thanks to you I became a...."

"You're Mairead Brennan's daughter. You know now you say it, I can see the family likeness. Fine woman. How are your parents?" Father Molloy asked.

"Pa died three years back. Mam decided to go back home to Ireland recently."

"I am very sorry for your loss. Your pa was a fine man. I must get your mam's address and write to her." He looked about him, presumably for something to write on.

Erin reached in her bag and taking a piece of paper and a pencil quickly wrote it for him.

She stood up to go.

"Don't be going just yet. It's marvelous to see you. How did you get on in medical school? Was it hard being a woman?" The priest stopped and laughed at himself. "Listen to me. I sound like Mary Sullivan." He stood up too.

"I was on my way to visit my friend Wilma at the orphanage. Why don't you come with me?" he suggested reaching for his hat. "We will get a nice cup of coffee and if we are lucky a cookie or two. Wilma is a rare character. You will like her."

Erin wasn't sure she wanted to go anywhere with the priest. He was bound to ask questions but it would be difficult to decline his invitation without sounding churlish.

"Sounds lovely, thank you, Father."

As they walked down the street, he explained he had been staying with Reverend Timmons and his wife while Mrs. Sullivan got ready for her influx of guests. "I heard on the grapevine some people thought you were one of our new waitresses."

"Yes, it was funny in hindsight. They seemed to think I was searching for a husband."

"I am sure you had at least a dozen proposals that first day. We are a small but growing community here in Clover Springs. It is a pleasant town although not as nice as it was six months or so ago."

She caught him glancing in the direction of the road leading to the saloon. She wasn't surprised. Most priests she knew didn't approve of drinking clubs.

* * *

"Wilma, are you at home?" he called as he opened the door to a building and walked right in.

"Where else would I be when you ming for your coffee?"

Erin was a bit taken aback by the gruff tone. Father Molloy let her walk in first. The woman's face was a picture.

"Oh Lordy me. I is ever so sorry, miss. I didn't know Father Molloy was bringing a stranger to visit." The woman threw Father Molloy a look.

"That's quite all right." Erin murmured wishing she had stayed in the boarding house.

"Take a seat Doc. Wilma will recover her manners in a minute to pour you the best cup of coffee in Colorado."

"You can stop your flannel you old goat. Excuse me. Did he call you Doc? You is the lady doctor everyone be talking about. Sure I thought you be as old as Mrs. Grey not some skinny young thing." Wilma put her hands on her hips, looking Erin up and down.

Erin burst out laughing. Father Molloy joined her.

"See I told you she was a character. Woman, are you going to pour the coffee or stand there making a show of yourself."

Wilma poured three cups of coffee still muttering under her breath. She put a plate of warm cookies in the middle of the table. The delicious smell made Erin's stomach growl.

"Oh please excuse me." Mortified, Erin didn't know where to look.

"You help yourself. Mrs. Grey, she done tole me all about you. You did a fine job with poor Hans. You can have as many cookies as you want." Turning her attention to Father Molloy, she said, "You can have one."

"That's not fair. Why you picking on me? I ain't done nothing." Father Molloy spoke like a child caught doing something wrong making the ladies laugh again.

"So what bring you to Clover Springs Missy? I heard we weren't expecting no doctor." Wilma looked from Erin to the priest and back.

"She came to see me. See I do have friends," Father Molloy answered.

"You? Why would a young girl come to see an old fool like you?" Wilma's hand caressed the priest's arm so Erin knew she was teasing him. She loved the way the woman and the priest interacted. It wasn't a bit like anything she was used to in New York. There the priests seldom smiled and certainly not at her. She was a sinner in their eyes. Shrugging those thoughts away she answered Wilma.

"My mam had a present for Father Molloy. I was on my way to a town the other side of Denver. Mam asked me to drop it off in person."

"She don't trust the postal system?" Wilma said smiling. "Good news for us. I hope you plan on visiting for a while."

"Erin just finished medical school, isn't that wonderful. I married her Mam and Da. God rest his soul. He was a fireman wasn't he Erin?"

"Yes, Father."

"A fireman? With a daughter at medical school. Miracles can happen," Wilma said.

"Because of Father Molloy. Mam told me he asked his parishioners to help and they did. I will always be grateful to you, Father."

"No need for gratitude. I am glad I could help." The priest looked embarrassed by her gratitude.

"We all end up in Clover Springs because of this man, one way or another. He's a good one even if he does preach too long," Wilma said smiling at the priest who blushed harder.

"Oh, that reminds me of my sermon. I never did find it. I have to go write another one."

"You need to find your own house and get yourself a housekeeper. Poor Mrs. Timmons, she ain't got time to be tidying up after you. Didn't I read in the bible that neatness was next to Godliness?"

Erin waited for a reaction to what most priests would consider blasphemy. She was sure the priest would start praying or screaming at Wilma.

Instead, Father Molloy nearly choked, he laughed so much.

"I wish Mrs. Grey was here to see you try and quote the bible, Wilma. You know that it doesn't say anything of the sort. Although a house is a good idea. The Timmons are rather stuck for space especially since Tilly moved in."

"The Timmons adopted Tilly, she was one of the thirty orphans Father Molloy's brought to Clover Springs last Christmas. She is a real peach." Wilma reached over to pour more coffee into Erin's cup. "You fire ahead, Father and write your sermon. Doc Erin can stay visiting with me for a while. I can pick her brains about how I am supposed to care for all these children."

"I hear you, Wilma. We are trying to find homes but it isn't easy. You know life is hard for people around here. And about to get harder if the news about cattle prices is anything to go by."

Father Molloy turned to Erin. "Thank you for my gift and it was lovely to see you. I will catch up properly with you someday soon but I best get to writing the sermon. For some reason, people groan if I talk too long." He winked.

"What you saying? You always talk too long. That's why people prefer it when Rev Timmons is doing the sermon. He is much faster."

"He has a wife waiting with a lovely home cooked meal," Father Molloy responded quickly.

"If that's your way of angling an invitation to my dinner table you can do better than that," Wilma retorted just as fast.

The priest left. They could still hear him laughing even after the door was closed.

"No better man alive than that one," Wilma said when her own laughter subsided.

"He isn't like any priest I know," Erin added.

"And ain't that the truth, thank God. Can't be doing with those who spend all their time looking down their noses at us mere mortals. I reckon God wanted those that lead us to be more like Father Molloy. Rev Timmons, he be a good man too but he don't got the same drive Father Molloy has for helping folk. Don't get me wrong. Rev Timmons would never turn away anyone in need, but he ain't about to go into the types of places Father Molloy goes either."

Erin didn't comment, she had met Reverend Timmons briefly when he was summoned to Mr. Hofmeister bedside.

"So do you like Clover Springs so far? A bit different from what you are used to I take it?" Wilma asked.

Surprised Erin asked. "How do you know?"

"People who dress like you don't usually live in

places like Clover Springs. You are like Alicia. She came with the orphans last Christmas. She is married now and has two boys. She adopted two of the orphans. I will introduce you to her the next time she comes to town."

"Thank you, Wilma."

"So what made you become a doctor?"

Erin spent a wonderful morning with Wilma. She told her all about her charity work with the Ellis Island immigrants while they peeled and sliced potatoes for the children's dinner. Wilma worked quickly, Erin less so but the older woman didn't seem to mind. She said she appreciated the company. "Don't get me wrong, I love my babies but they ain't such good conventionalists."

CHAPTER 15

Sullivan Ranch

"What's eating you?"

"Nothing." Mick hoped Cookie would leave him alone. He didn't want to talk about anything right now.

"So why did you just take the nose off young Ben's face. You know he looks up to you."

"Ain't nothing to look up to," Mick growled. He felt bad about Ben. The youngster had come a long way since Miss Mary had adopted him but at times you could see the hurt little boy who nobody wanted. Like about an hour ago when he'd snapped at him. Ben hadn't done anything wrong either apart from ask him how it was in town.

Cookie stared and waited.

"I'll find him in a bit and say sorry. That make you happy."

"Yup, for Ben. Not what got you into this mood. I told you to leave the whiskey in the bottle. That the only place for it."

"Cooke don't start on your lectures. I didn't have that much to drink."

Cookies look said it all. "Your bunk was all neat and tidy this morning."

"It's always like that," Mick replied.

"Not in the middle of the night it ain't. Where were you?"

"Jeez, Cookie you're not my ma and I ain't a kid. Back off will you."

Cookie moved away grumbling, banging pots, letting Mick know he wasn't happy. Mick knew he should have just said he stayed in town but then he'd have to answer more questions. He couldn't do that. All he could see was Mollie's face as she slept.

He pushed back his chair. He had to go find Ben and then he was going back into town.

He found Ben in the stables where he was brushing down his horse The look of misery on Ben's face made Mick feel even worse. "Ben, look about earlier-"

"No need to say anything. I know when I am not wanted."

"Will you quit bellyaching. You ain't a snotty nosed

kid. I came to apologize. I had something on my mind. Nothing to do with you, Son. I shouldn't have bit your head off."

Ben looked up and then he smiled. "I get a bit cross too sometimes. Ma says I am not a morning person."

Mick ruffled Ben's hair. "I think your ma might have a lot to say about my mood. Let's not tell her I upset you. I could do without one of Mary Sullivan's lectures right now."

They both smiled. Mary was known for her protective streak, especially when it came to Ben. She was right too. The young boy had suffered enough. His own family had abandoned him for being a cripple and the Nuns in the orphanage hadn't treated him much better. Cookie reckoned the reason Ben followed Mick around when he came back from a drive was Mick could do everything he wanted and he limped too.

"So how's the training going? Is she learning how to run rope yet?" Mick asked the youngster.

"She already knows that. I could show you only Pa won't let me. He said it's too dangerous. But all the other boys my age do it."

Mick knew what Davy was afraid of. The polio had left Ben's legs weak, one in particular was twisted. You needed your leg strength to stay on the horse. He was afraid something bad would happen. But there was no point in explaining that to Ben. He just wanted to be like one of the other boys.

"I'll have a word with your pa. I'll also catch up with Little Beaver in town later and see if he can talk the boss around. Davy listens to Little Beaver especially when it comes to horses."

Ben grin grew wider making Mick feel less guilty.

"Don't be saying anything yet though. You don't want your Ma getting wind of it, or I will be the one riding off in the sunset."

Ben shook his head. "I won't say nothing. Thanks, Mick."

He took Mick by surprise by throwing his arms around him for a hug. Stunned at first, Mick found himself hugging him back thinking there wasn't that much age difference between Mollie and Ben. Yet their circumstances couldn't be more different. Well, financially anyway. Inside, they both shared a lot of the same hurts.

What was the matter with him? He was goin' real soft in his old age.

"Ben I got to go now. I got to be somewhere." He walked toward the bunkhouse.

"Yeah, I know. The Red Feathers."

Mick stopped. "What did you say?"

"Sorry, Mick. It slipped out."

Mick was annoyed, not with the boy. Ben had

obviously heard chatter from the men. They had better things to be doing than talking about his visits to the saloon.

"I'll see you tomorrow, Ben. Now get that horse seen to."

"Goodnight Mick, thanks."

Mick walked slowly back to the bunkhouse. His leg was giving him grief. It did that in the cold weather but also when he was pushing it too hard. He rubbed his hand along his thigh. He never let anyone see the extent of the damage. He'd been lucky to be taken to the Union hospital. If he'd gone to the other, he'd have been left to die or, worse, had his leg amputated. The skill of the Yankee surgeon had saved not only his life but his leg. The surgeon had also seen him for what he was, a thirteen-year-old boy not a soldier. It was he who introduced him to Cookie. They'd been together since.

Mick tried to apologize to Cookie, too, but he got the silent treatment. Only the increased banging of the plates and pots meant the older man had heard him. Mick sighed and headed back out again. He had to make sure Mollie was all right. He didn't trust Dickie not one little bit.

CHAPTER 16

Erin carried her bag as she lifted her skirts with her other hand making her way carefully down the street. Thank goodness the boardwalk covered most of her journey. As she walked, she tried to think of different ways to convince Mrs. Hofmeister she needed to stay in Clover Springs. At least until the baby was born but preferably for a while afterwards. She spotted children further up the street heading, she guessed, to school. She wondered what their teacher was like.

She arrived at the mill. It was still working although there were fewer men around today than previously. They must have worked through most of the orders by now.

Knocking on the door, she called out to Mrs.

Hofmeister as she walked inside. Hearing no answer, she was about to leave when she heard a slight moan. Mrs. Hofmeister was sitting on the kitchen floor.

"What happened? Is it the baby?" Erin asked as she crouched over her.

"No. Not baby but my head. I was dizzy and fell over."

Erin helped her to her feet, settling her in a chair before she gave her a thorough examination. She seemed okay but judging by the weary look on her face she wasn't getting enough rest. "You need to rest." She mimed the actions of sleeping in case the woman didn't understand.

"I cannot rest. I have to pack and make plans. I..."

"You cannot go anywhere not until the baby comes," Erin spoke harshly without intending to.

Terror-stricken the woman started to cry. "I cannot stay here. I don't have enough money. No family. I have to go."

She tried to stand up but Erin made her sit back down again. "You are not leaving Clover Springs. Now go back to bed. I will make you breakfast and bring it to you. You are not to get out of bed until I come back. Do you understand?"

Meekly the woman nodded her head. She lead the way to her bedroom such as it was. Erin helped her lie on the bed before going back to the kitchen. There was very little food making Erin think she had been feeding her child and possibly starving herself in the process. She fried up an egg and some bread and brought it back to the pregnant mother. Mrs. Hofmeister had already fallen asleep. Erin hated to wake her but she needed to eat more than sleep. She waited until the lady ate everything before letting her fall back asleep again.

Erin closed the door of the house gently behind her. It was time to call on Mrs. Grey and see what she could do to help.

Mrs. Grey was out on a call to another pregnant lady. Emer suggested she go speak to Katie Sullivan at the store.

Erin pushed open the store door relieved to see it was empty she didn't want to discuss Mrs. Hofmeister's private business in public. A smiling young lady stood behind the counter, holding a young toddler in her arms.

"Sorry he's cutting teeth and it's making him rather grouchy. I'm Katie. You are Erin Brennan, aren't you? Don't look so surprised news travels fast in the small town."

“Pleased to meet you. Mrs. Shipley suggested I come and speak to you,” Erin said politely.

“Emer, you mean? Oh no, am I in trouble?”

Erin smiled, "Not exactly but I need your help. Well more specifically, Mrs. Hofmeister needs help."

"That was a horrible tragedy. Hans Hofmeister was a lovely man. Not that I knew him long but he was always pleasant when he came into the shop. Can't say that for all our customers."

Erin took a deep breath hoping the kind woman would be able to help. "Mrs. Hofmeister's baby is due very soon but she plans to go to live in Kansas. I can't have her traveling that far not after the shock she's had."

"But she can't afford to say here without an income," Katie added.

"Yes, that's it exactly."

Katie stayed silent a moment before speaking. "Could you take Danny for a minute please?" Katie handed Erin her toddler. She held the baby close, savoring the feeling. Meanwhile, Katie moved quickly collecting a few essential items from around the store, placing them in a bundle on the counter.

"This is just a start. I will have it delivered to Mrs. Hofmeiser. She will believe Han's had credit in the store."

"Thank you for your kindness, Katie. Mrs. Shipley was right to tell me to call on you."

Katie blushed as she took Danny back into her arms. "Why don't you come to our quilting circle,

Erin. The ladies might be able to help. They usually have plenty of ideas."

Erin thought of her mam and her sewing buddies.

"Thank you, it would be nice to meet some of the ladies of the town."

CHAPTER 17

Mick wandered into the saloon trying to look casual. After ordering a beer, he took a look around delighted to see Dickie sitting alone at a table. He walked toward it but another man blocked his way.

"Let him through."

"Sure thing, boss." The man stood to let Mick pass.

"What can I do for you, cowboy?"

"How much do you want for Mollie's contract?" Micke asked.

"You got it bad, cowboy." Dickie's twisted grin made Mick want to hit him very hard. He kept his fists clenched by his side, he couldn't afford to lose his temper. Mollie would end up paying the price.

"How much?"

"Why her? I have a new shipment coming into Leadville soon. Some young girls with less... baggage."

Mick swallowed the bile in his throat as he caught the meaning. He could have easily wrung Dickie's neck but that wasn't going to help Mollie.

"Are you going to chat all day or answer the question. I have things to do."

"Two hundred."

Mick knew he hadn't hidden his dismay when Dickie laughed and stood up. "Let me buy you a drink. You need a bit of color in your cheeks."

Mick didn't want a drink but he wasn't about to say no. It was dangerous. Dickie knew of his interest in Mollie. It may lead the girl into danger. It could also mean Dickie didn't mistreat her. One look into Dickie's eyes told Mick that was too much to hope for. The black eyes staring back at him had no life, no emotion. They could have been discussing the price of a mule for all it mattered. Mick emptied his glass in one gulp and stalked out.

He marched down the street his mind going over and over. He didn't have that type of money. Could he borrow it? The farm was probably worth a good bit now. But he'd sworn he would only use the farm to help his sisters.

* * *

He rode past the jailhouse relieved to see the light on. Dismounting, he tied his horse to the post and made his way inside. Little Beaver looked up as the door closed. "I was just about to go on my round. The Sheriff will be back in a minute."

"Can I come with you? I need to talk."

Mick waited as Little Beaver securitized his face before nodding. "We wait for the Sheriff."

The sheriff wasn't long. He tried to entice Mick to stay in the warmth and have some coffee. Tempting although that was Mick wanted to find out what Little Beaver knew about Dickie.

They walked through the town in silence for a little while.

"You know I am not medicine man in my people."

Surprised, Mick looked at the Indian to see him smiling. "I cannot read minds. Tell me what the trouble is and I can help."

"How do you know it's trouble?" Mick said.

"You do not need to be a mind reader to see real sadness in your face. Not past sadness that is always there but this is new."

"It's Ben. And Davy." He immediately felt guilty as concern filled Little Beaver's face.

"What is wrong? Are they sick?"

Sorry, he had caused his friend concern, Mick hastened to reassure him. "Ben wants to ride out with the cattle and Davy won't let him. I understand why but it's hurting Ben."

"It is because Davy and Mary think Ben will get hurt."

"I know that," Mick retorted.

Little Beavers expression changed at Mick's tone.

"Sorry, didn't mean to snap," Mick apologized. "Haven't been sleeping too well. What I mean is I know the risks but Ben is growing up fast. They can't keep him from being a man."

"Being able to ride a horse does not a man make."

At Mick's snort, Little Beaver stopped walking and crossed his hands over his chest. "This is not to do with Ben. This black mood of yours is to do with something lot more than Ben. Yes?"

"There are lots of reasons for my mood but Ben is the one I need help with. Can you talk to Davy?"

"Me?" Little Beaver raised his eyebrow.

"Yes, you. He respects you and there is no one who knows horses better. I can try but well..."

"After you tried to steal his woman…"

"I never, oh you." Mick stopped as Little Beaver started laughing.

"We will talk to Davy together. I will tell him to let Ben ride, you will promise you will look after Ben like your own child."

Mick nodded.

"Now Ben is sorted, what about Mick?"

Mick didn't want to talk so started walking leaving Little Beaver standing. He thought Little Beaver would follow him but he didn't, making Mick walk back to him. "You coming or you going to stand here all night?"

"You tell me what is eating you in here," Little Beaver pointed to his heart, "and I will come."

Mick knew when he was beaten. "How much do you know about Dickie at the Red Feathers?"

Little Beavers face turned sour right before his eyes. "I do not like that man. He should be forced to leave Clover Springs."

"Has he done something? Can you make it happen?" Mick asked hopefully.

"No. He has done a lot of bad things. The smell follows him around. But I have no proof. The sheriff says we cannot act without it. Dickie is a powerful man. He has what you call connections."

Mick stayed silent. It was just as he feared

"You have reason to be scared of this man?" Little Beaver asked.

"Not me."

"A woman?"

"She's not really a woman, more of a child. She works in the saloon."

"Ah, you mean Mollie."

Surprised, Mick stopped walking. “How do you know her?”

“Wilma told me about her. Asked me to keep a watch for her when I make my rounds. I cannot go inside the saloon. My kind is not welcome.”

Mick didn’t know why he confided in Little Beaver. The words came out of his mouth before he could stop them. “Dickie told me I could buy Mollie's contract for two hundred dollars.”

“Why?”

“I have no idea how he came to that figure. I guess she earns ...”

“No. Why Mollie?” Little Beaver scrutinized him so closely, Mick was convinced the Indian could read his mind.

“She reminds me of someone.” He hoped Little Beaver would let the matter drop.

“Your child?”

Mick spluttered. “My what? I don’t have any kids.”

Little Beaver shrugged. “The town folk think you do. They say it is why you go away so much.”

“Well, they are wrong. I ain’t got kids and I never going to have them neither.” Mick's hand unconsciously strayed to his upper leg.

Little Beaver didn’t seem to notice. "Being father is best feeling. Brown fox is very clever boy."

"He's nine months old." Mick smiled at his friend’s

proud face. Little Beaver was very much the doting father.

"He will be more clever when he is older. Strong too."

They'd arrived outside the saloon. Mick looked inside and saw Mollie. She seemed to be looking for someone. Her eyes scanned the crowd until she came to his face. Then her smile brightened. She waved but her smile faded as he stayed outside.

"She looks like she was expecting you."

"I stayed here last night." Mick couldn't believe he admitted that out loud. The look of displeasure was back on Little Beaver's face.

"I will leave you now. I have work to do."

"It wasn't like that. Nothing happened." But Mick was talking to his friend's back.

He felt like stamping the floor in temper. Instead, he pushed open the door of the saloon and headed straight for the bar. A shot or two would help chase the demons away.

CHAPTER 18

Mollie was at his side almost the same time as he reached the bar.

"I hoped you'd come back tonight."

"I'm sorry, Mollie, I only came in for a drink. I have to get back to the ranch."

He felt so bad watching her face fall. He had only made things much worse by being nice to her. Showing her hope and taking it away from her was cruel. She turned to go. He took her arm.

"Why don't we share that drink?"

He bought two beers tipping the barkeep in the process. If he wanted to find out what exactly was going on in this place, he would need some new friends. He walked over to a table and took a seat. Mollie sat on the chair beside him, nursing her drink, looking around her the whole time.

"What's got you so nervous?" he asked.

"Nothing."

"Mollie?"

"Dickie expects me to be working."

"You are working. I am paying you to drink with me."

A flush came to her face as she looked upstairs.

"Would you feel more comfortable?" he asked reluctantly, knowing the answer.

She nodded.

They took the drinks and moved slowly upstairs. As soon as the door closed, Mollie hugged Mick, spilling the drinks

"Is it true? What Dickie said?"

Oh, this was worse than he could have imagined.

"Mollie, I ... Well, I might have asked Dickie a question but I can't do anything. I don't have the type of money he's asking."

The look of disappointment on her face floored him.

"I am really sorry, Mollie."

"Don't matter, the girls said I was stupid to believe it anyway. Nothing good ever happens to girls like us."

"Don't say things like that, Mollie," he said although he knew it to be true.

"Why not, it's true. There is no future for me. I will be lucky to last here a couple of years. If I upset

Dickie he said he would send me to the cribs in Fort Worth."

Mick had to fight the urge to go find Dickie and kick the daylights out of him. Scaring a young girl like that was unforgivable. He knew about the cribs, what drover didn't. The thoughts of anyone ending up there was horrible but someone as young as Mollie didn't bear thinking about.

"Mollie, I am going to try and get you out of here. But it will take time. You will have to do whatever Dickie says in the meantime."

Mollie looked at him, he could see hope fighting with terror in her eyes.

"Can you hold me?" Mollie asked quietly.

Putting the drinks down he held his arms open closing the around her fragile body.

"Mollie, when you last saw a doctor?"

Her body stiffened within his arms.

"I don't need a doctor. I ain't sick."

"There is a new doctor in town. A lady one. You could, you know, ask her things." Mick was out of his depth talking about this kind of stuff. He hoped Mollie would understand what he was trying to say.

"Ask her what?"

"Just things. She could examine you too. Maybe she could get Dickie to give you more time to rest."

Mick knew he was desperate but it was worth a shot wasn't it. He didn't even know if the lady doctor would come near the saloon.

"Do you think it will help?" she asked quietly.

"Yes."

"Then I will do it. I'll do anything for you, Mick."

The hero worship in her eyes tore at his heart. She was so like Susanna, his baby sister. He hugged her close, his tears mingling with her hair. "I promise I will do all I can Mollie. I promise."

After a while, they drew apart.

"I best get back downstairs or Dickie will be looking for me," she said reluctantly.

"You wait here. I will pay Dickie for the night. You can rest."

The smile on her face was worth the hit to his wallet.

"Don't open the door until I get back."

She nodded, looking a little scared but determined.

He moved quickly downstairs to find Dickie. He spotted him playing cards with a group of nasty looking strangers. Mick didn't recognize any of them. He loosened the yoke holding his gun in just in case.

He knew Dickie saw him but the saloon owner made him wait like a lackey until he had played his hand.

"What can I do for you, Mick?"

Mick threw three dollars on the table. "I want to buy the whole night."

"Mollie again. She must surely be to your liking."

The crude laughter around the table made Mick's blood boil but he refused to let them see the effect they had.

"Who is Mollie? She isn't the young thing I had my eye on earlier?"

Mick met the eyes of the man speaking. He had a scar running down one side of his cheek and a matching one just under his chin. His eyes were cruel and twisted.

"Yes, that's the one. Told you she was popular," Dickie said, the ever-present cigar held in the corner of his mouth.

"But I thought I had her for the night. You promised."

The scared man went to stand up but a quick flick of Dickie's hand and two cowboys had their hands on his shoulder pushing him back into the chair.

"Didn't see you parting with any money, Rogers. This here cowboy got in first. This time."

Mick's blood turned to ice. This time. Mick couldn't afford to be here every night and they both knew it.

"Thanks, Dickie," he forced himself to say. Tipping his hat at the other men, he walked slowly back toward the stairs half expecting to feel something in his back.

CHAPTER 19

Mick lay on the bed on top of the covers while Mollie lay under them.

"Mick, will you cuddle me?"

He put his arm around her so she rested her head on his shoulder.

"Why do you treat me so nice?" she asked.

"You are a lovely girl, Mollie, you deserve it."

"That's sweet but it ain't the truth. I seen the way the women in the town look at me. That's if they do look at me."

"Don't mind anyone else. It's what you feel inside that's important. You are a human being Mollie," Mick replied trying to keep his anger at judgmental women under control.

"Why are you so different?"

Mick didn't know how to answer.

"You hush now and sleep."

"Mick, thank you." Mollie leaned up and kiss his cheek. "Even if you can't get me out of here, I will always remember your kindness."

She snuggled into him and fell fast asleep. He held her close. It was comforting to hold someone near. It reminded him of a time long past when his family used to gather around the fire and listen to Ma's stories or Pa playing his fiddle. He opened his eyes hoping to get rid of the images in his head. He could see his sisters faces as clear as day. He prayed hard they had been adopted by a nice family. Someday he would find them and they could be a family again. They might even have families of their own. He liked children.

Mick closed his eyes and drifted into a restless sleep. Dickie's face mingled with those of his parents and sisters. Then the war dreams started.

He woke suddenly, thrashing about. Mollie had jumped from the bed, holding her dress in front of her, her face a mask of terror.

"Sorry Mollie, I just get nightmares. Did I hit you?"

She moved to sit on the edge of the bed. "No, but you scared the life out of me with your yelling. What were you dreaming about?"

"The war."

"You been in the war? I didn't know you were that ... "She stopped speaking as she giggled. "I was going to call you old."

"To you, I am ancient. Lie back down. I got to get back to the ranch in time for breakfast."

He got up, too embarrassed to look at her. Putting his boots on, he grabbed his hat and headed out the door.

"Mick, thank you. You don't have to keep coming back. I know you ain't got a lot of money. I will be fine."

He glanced at her white face, her eyes huge dark holes of terror. She was trying so hard to be brave, poor kid. He had to help.

"I will see you soon Moll, take care."

He didn't look back as he exited the room. He moved quickly out of the building wanting to be free of the oppressive atmosphere. How many more girls were there like Mollie? You can't help them all. No, but I will be darned if I can't help Mollie.

* * *

He got back to the ranch before the other cowboys had got up. This time he remembered to screw up his bed covers as if he had slept all night. He headed for the creek. Despite the cold, he needed a wash. He had to get clean.

Cookie eyed him over breakfast. It was obvious he knew Mick had stayed out again all night but they didn't discuss it. They both had jobs to do, no time to stand around gossiping like two old women.

CHAPTER 20

There was a large turnout at the next town meeting. Erin sat near the back. Mrs. Grey had wanted her to sit up front beside her but Erin thought it best to keep a low profile.

"I don't think the town needs two doctors. And if we did, we would get a real one." Charlie Staunton's chest stuck out so much, Mrs. Grey thought it might burst. A few of the townsfolk agreed with him if their nodding heads was anything to go by.

"Erin is a real doctor. She graduated from one of the top medical schools."

'You only have her word for that."

"Mr. Staunton, there is no need to be rude. You are entitled to your opinion, misguided though it might be please mind your manners," Mrs. Grey said coldly.

"Why don't we ask the Doc what he thinks? He's

qualified and he's the one who will have to share the work," Katie suggested.

"Thank you, Katie. Personally, I am thrilled and more than a little excited to be working with someone of Doc Brennan's caliber. It's been a long time since I left medical school and my skills are rather rusty."

"Don't agree there, Doc. I think we keep you so busy, you ain't got time to rust," Davy shouted out.

"I think it's wonderful if Clover Springs hires a female doctor. We are sending a message we are a progressive town. Kansas has a female mayor," Mrs. Grey continued.

"Well, this ain't Kansas and the only place a woman should be is in the home. That's my opinion anyway and I ain't never going to change it."

"Thankfully the decision isn't yours to make Mr. Staunton," Mrs. Grey said dismissively. "We have to agree or disagree in the majority. I think we should make a show of hands."

"Before we do that, there is something I would like to add to the discussion." Father Molloy stood up. He wiped his hands down the front of his clothes, something he always did when he was nervous. What shock has he got for us now? Mrs. Grey wondered but she stayed silent, waiting for the priest to speak.

"As you know, we are working on getting more single women to come and live in Clover Springs. It is our hope we will be able to provide a means of hope and employment to those who probably have neither."

"What's that got to do with the doctor?" Staunton shouted.

Father Molloy ignored him

"Some of the ladies who come to us for help may have experienced, well let's just say they may have a past." Father Molloy's face was scarlet. Mrs. Grey felt very sorry for him.

"I knew it. You are going to bring in more of those wanton women who work in the saloon," Mrs. Shaw said triumphantly.

"Those so-called wanton women have a need for love and kindness as well as medical attention. The women I am talking about may have been the subject of certain events. They may benefit from seeing a female doctor."

Poor Father Molloy, he was getting tongue twisted trying not to offend anyone.

"What the man is trying to say is that there are some women out there that ain't never going to trust another man no matter what he may be. Doctor, priest, reverend, it won't matter. All they will see is he's a man." Wilma looked around her. "That be right, ain't it Father."

"Yes Wilma, thank you for putting my thoughts into words." Father Molloy smiled as everyone laughed. Wilma took a bow and sat back down in her seat.

"It isn't just those ladies who may benefit. Sometimes it would be nice to discuss certain issues with another woman. No offense Doc." Mrs. Larkin glanced at the town doctor.

"None taken Mrs. Larkin. I often find myself wishing my patients were talking to a woman." Everyone laughed again. Doc was known for his impatience for chatting or gossiping as he liked to call it.

"Has anyone asked the doctor? I mean the lady doc?" Mick's ears turned bright pink as he asked his question.

"What's it got to do with her. It's the towns decision to make and she ain't part of the town," Staunton answered before Mrs. Grey had time to react.

"I think she has a right to decide if she wants to live here or not. If she is dead set on going to Denver or somewhere else then our conversation is pretty pointless," Mick retorted.

"If she's set on Denver, we should help her on her way. As I said, nobody in this territory going trust a woman doc. You wait and see. She will be sitting doing her knitting all day long."

"I certainly hope that isn't the case. I am very bad at knitting."

Everyone sat stunned as Erin made her way to the top of the room.

"I think it would be a good idea if I talk to you all just as I would for any job interview. You can ask me questions and I will do my best to answer them."

"Will you marry me?" A cowboy shouted out from the back of the crowd.

"Not this year, I am rather busy," she quipped back. She surveyed the room. "Has anyone a serious question? Perhaps you, sir, as you seem to have already made your mind up."

Charlie Staunton didn't answer.

"Would you be willing to stay in Clover Springs if you were offered a position here?" Mick surprised himself by asking. A few of the cowboys around him nudged him and started whispering but he ignored them. His gaze locked on hers. He watched as she rubbed the side of her neck. She was nervous.

"Yes, I would consider it subject to certain criteria."

'She wants a large paycheck," Charlie Staunton shouted.

"I expect to be fairly rewarded for my efforts but that is not the most important consideration."

"What's more important than money?" Staunton scoffed as he looked around the room.

"Respect. In as far as I am able, I would prefer not to have to treat those patients who have no belief in my ability to practice medicine. I would like the current town doctor to take those patients."

"I thought I liked you, Doc Brennan." The doctor's irony was lost on many people but not on Mick.

"I should like to specialize in childcare. There are so many things we can do to help children grow up healthier and stronger. Having seen the effects of poor diet, lack of sanitation and fresh air back in New York, I would like to do something in that area," Erin continued.

"Now you are talking. Far too many children coming to see me. Some of them want to sit on my knee of all things." The doctor's protests were funny as everyone who knew him knew he kept a bag of candy in his pocket. He loved children.

"Why don't we give it a trial run? Doc Brennan, you have nothing to lose. You said yourself you haven't yet found a position in Denver. Maybe having a few months of experience working in a town like this would help future applications. Clover Springs can see women can make excellent doctors as well as lawyers, judges and ..." Mrs. Grey was rudely interrupted.

"Now wait a minute, Mrs. Grey this is one of your crusades. We are here to vote on whether we offer the new doctor a job or not," Charlie Staunton roared.

Mrs. Grey gracefully nodded.

* * *

ERIN THOUGHT she saw a spark of triumph in the older woman's eyes. She was very good at getting what she wanted, something Erin could do with remembering.

The voting closed with a narrow majority in favor of keeping Erin on as a doctor. She was more than a little disappointed. The number of people who opposed a female doctor was high.

"Don't be disappointed, Erin. It's a different place out here from that you are used to in New York or I was in Boston. The people here aren't used to seeing women in everyday occupations like we are." Alicia said.

"Everything is still handled by men. Even the store is owned by Daniel although we are hoping Katie will take the hint and open her own dress shop soon," Emer Shipley added.

"Katie Sullivan has enough to be doing taking care of her husband and two children. She doesn't need any more projects."

"Doc Erin, this is my husband, Daniel Sullivan. Excuse yourself dear or Doc Erin will think I married an ape."

Erin smiled at the interaction between the couple it reminded her of her mam and da. The smile faded as the man who had obstructed her appointment so loudly walked over.

"You may have won the first round, lady, but you will soon find out your sort aren't welcome here."

"Don't listen to him. He must have a very serious case of hemorrhoids. He is so bad-tempered. It is the only excuse," Mrs. Grey said taking Erin's elbow and leading her out the door.

Erin heard the man's panicky question to the old doctor.

"What did Mrs. Grey say I have? How come you never told me I had a serious disease," Staunton demanded but before the doctor got a chance to answer, Emer did.

"Piles." Emer Shipley translated for him.

Erin turned around in time to see Charlie Staunton's going as red as some of the ladies present as all the men laughed at his discomfort.

"Next time you need to get on a horse, call me and I will help you up." One of the cowboys shouted, making Charlie go even redder.

Erin left the building with a smile on her face. She hadn't been here long but already she had made some great friends.

CHAPTER 21

Mick Quinn stood at the door to the orphanage kitchen. He watched Wilma as she worked for a couple of seconds trying to gather his thoughts together.

"You going stand there all day?" Wilma asked.

"Miss Wilma, can I have a word?" Mick asked, holding his hat in his hands.

"Do you want coffee and cookies with it?" Wilma asked smiling at him.

"Only if you made them yourself. "

'"I sure did. It must be something big you have on your mind to be wastin' your Irish charm on me, boy. Take the weight off your legs and sit down."

Mick sat at the table twisting the cup this way and that.

"Mick, you gonna spill that coffee everywhere. I

got enough work to do. Now tell me what's on your mind."

Mick looked into the big brown eyes full of kindness and concern. He was overwhelmed with shame that he had once fought on the side determined to keep this good woman and people like her in slavery.

"Wilma, there's something you should know first before I ask for your help."

"What's that then?" Wilma barely looked up from arranging the cookies on the plate.

"I fought in the war."

"I knows that already."

"Yeah, but I fought on the Confederacy side."

A quick hiss as Wilma sucked her breath in was the only reaction. He waited a couple of seconds to see what she would say but she stayed silent.

"My daddy got killed and they said I had to fight in his place. I didn't know much about the war. We didn't own slaves or nothing. We didn't have the money."

"Would you have owned slaves if you had the money. Be honest with me," Wilma stared right into his eyes. He didn't flinch.

"No Ma'am. Ma always told us all people is the same. No matter what color they be."

"Well then, sounds like your ma and me would have been good friends. What age were you when you went fighting 'cause you look mighty young to be a war veteran?"

"Thirteen ma'am," Mick replied quietly.

"You was nothing but a child. Them men was wrong to take you to war. But I'm guessing you ain't here to talk about the war. What can I do for you?"

"There's this girl."

Wilma let out a deep throaty laugh. "There's always a girl involved in a man's troubles."

He didn't laugh so she faltered, "You got a girl in trouble."

"Yes, at least I think so."

"Don't you sit there telling me you think so. You might have been a boy when you went fighting but you is a man now. You can do better than that. This girl, does her family know she going to have your baby?"

Shocked at the force of her temper, Mick nearly fell backward off his chair as Wilma poked her finger in his face.

"It ain't like that. There's no baby," he stuttered trying to keep his balance.

"I ain't following you."

"That's cause you ain't listening. You speaking too much and shaking your finger in my face. I ain't no schoolboy. I came for your help, not a lecture," Mick growled.

Wilma sat back. "Sorry Mick, my temper gets too hot on occasion. Let's start again. A girl needs help because of something you did."

Mick didn't meet her eyes, he couldn't as he felt too guilty. "It's one of Dickie's girls."

"You here talking to me about a soiled dove?" Wilma's tone wasn't shocked as much as surprised.

"It's Mollie. I know you know her, she told me you were nice to her."

A shadow flitted over Wilma's face.

"Yeah, I know her. What you done to Mollie? You hurt her?" Wilma's temper was rising again.

"Yeah, but not in the way you mean. I gave her hope and then took it away. I was so stupid."

"Mick tell me the whole story from the start."

So Mick told her about paying for two nights just so Mollie could sleep. He told her about his conversation with Dickie, wincing at the look on her face as he related the details.

"I ain't got that type of money or no way to get it," Mick said, his desperation evident.

"I ain't got it either, son."

"I know that Wilma, but I got to find a way to get it. I can't bear to think of her face. If I had left her alone from the start, she wouldn't have even thought about leaving her life."

Wilma took his hand, "Mick Quinn, you look

here and listen good. She'll have been thinking of ways of leaving that life from the moment it started. Make no mistake. You were kind to her. That's a good thing. Do you know how few men think of girls like Mollie as people? You made her feel like a human being for a few hours. That was a real good thing. Don't you tell yourself different." Wilma tapped the table to illustrate her point. Mick knew she was trying to make him feel better but it wasn't working.

"It's not enough though. I asked Little Beaver if he could help but he said the Sheriff says there is nothing the law can do. They don't have anything they can stick on Dickie."

Wilma stood up to get more coffee. With her back to him, Mick thought he heard sniffles but he wasn't sure. By the time she turned around, there were no signs of tears.

"You know people fought us hard when we wanted to open this orphanage. They fought us real hard when Father Molloy and Alicia brought out all the orphans," Wilma stopped to take a breath. "Yet Dickie and his friends can run a house like that and nobody says anything to stop him. I don't understand it."

"People look the other way when it comes to Mollie and girls like her," Mick said although he was pointing out the obvious.

"Why are you so different? What makes Mollie special? You in love with her?"

Mick nearly choked on his coffee. "Wilma she's just a kid. I ain't like that."

"So why her?" Wilma persisted. "There are a million Mollies out there."

"I don't know." Mick decided it was time to leave. The conversation was becoming very uncomfortable.

"Mick Quinn you is lying to me now. I don't like liars. I am going to try my best to help you and Mollie but you got to tell me the truth. Why her?"

Mick stared at Wilma for some time. What did he have to lose by telling the truth? It would show his weak spot but this was Wilma. She'd never use the knowledge against him. Suddenly he felt he had to tell her the whole story.

"She reminds me of someone."

"Who?"

Mick gulped hard past the lump in his throat. He reached into his pocket and took out the dog eared photograph passing it to Wilma. She looked at it closely for a few minutes.

"This here be your family?"

Mick nodded.

"You all look happy."

"We were. Ma and Pa are gone now."

"And the little girls."

"I don't know where they are. I came back from the Yankee hospital in 1866 and there was nothing left. No farm, no house and no..."

He couldn't finish.

Wilma kept silent looking at the photo.

"They be real pretty. What ages would they be now?"

"About twenty-seven. If they are still alive. I don't know what happened to them."

"I can see why Mollie reminds you of them. She looks a bit like them. But your sisters were most likely adopted into a lovely family. They could have families of their own now."

"Don't Wilma. I know you are trying to be nice but we both know the type of things that happened in that war. It's still going on now."

Wilma didn't answer. He guessed she was thinking of her own family assuming she had one. She was bound to have had brothers and sisters or maybe a husband and babies of her own. Something stopped him from asking. Wilma never spoke about her past. Not to anyone, not even Miss Laura and they were closer than anything.

"Cookie saved me. I wasn't fit for nothing after the war. I was so sure I would go home and they'd be there waiting. Cookie helped me get the farm back up and running. It was hard going but the land was good. Pa chose a good place. Every day I looked down the road hoping to see the girls coming. But nothing. Nobody knew anything. A few years went by. I had to get away. Cookie found a family willing to rent the farm and we took to the road doing odd jobs here and there. Suited us both. We searched every town, chased down every lead but nothing."

"This family you rented your farm to. Are they still living there?" Wilma asked.

"Yes. That's where I go every summer. Stupid really as they would send a telegram if they had any news. They want to buy the farm now. It's a good one. But I can't let go of it. It's not just my home, it's my sister's home too. And Cookies."

Wilma reached over to pat his hand but kept her eyes averted from his face. He rubbed his sleeve over his eyes thankful for her discretion.

"You got to look forward not back Mick. You can't spend your life living in the past. Believe me that don't work. I knows from experience, it only leads to more heartbreak."

The two sat in silence for a while before Mick pushed back his chair. "I got to go. Promised I would help out at the mill."

"Its real nice of you to help Mrs. Hofmeister. The poor lady."

"Davy is the nice one, he gave us the time off to

help. Hopefully, she will have enough cash to keep her going when the little one comes."

Something in Wilma's face prompted his next question. "What?"

"Seems like Hans borrowed some money to expand his business. Mrs. Hofmeister has quite a big debt to pay off."

"Can't Shipley do something. Surely that bank of his doesn't need any more profit." Even as he made the comment, he knew it was unfair. He had never heard anything but good things about Lawrence Shipley.

"It ain't the bank she owes money to. Mr. Lawrence, he tried to talk Hans out of the loan and said no. But..."

"Hans borrowed it anyway. From who?" Mick asked despite knowing he wouldn't like the answer.

Wilma stayed quiet.

Mick felt sick asking "Not Dickie?"

Wilma nodded. "Seems Mrs. Hofmeister has been offered a couple of ways of paying off the loan."

"Of all the dirty low down dogs. He is lower than a rattlesnake." Mick fisted his hands.

"Don't you get yourself in the middle of it. There's other people helping Mrs. Hofmeister. You got to stay away from Dickie. From what you told me, he knows your weak spot."

Mollie. Anything he did to Dickie, she would pay.

"What is a creep like him doing here in Clover Springs anyway?"

"I don't know but I reckon it's about time he got moved on. Clover Springs is a nice place to live and I want it to stay that way. I going to talk to the Reverend about calling another town meeting."

"The town is more likely to help Mrs. Hofmeister than Mollie. Her being a respectable widow and everything." Mick knew he sounded bitter.

"You would think so but Mrs. Hofmeister is German and there isn't much love around some people for what they consider foreigners," Wilma said sadly. She stood up, taking the dishes in her hands. "Anyway if we get rid of Dickie, it will help both won't it?"

Mick grinned for the first time since calling to see Wilma. "There's a reason why everyone likes you so much. You find a way around everything."

"With my history, you had to. Now go on, you ain't the only one with chores to do. I got to get a meal ready for the children they be hungry when they get out of school."

Mick was at the door when Wilma said softly, "Thank you for sharing your family with me. I won't tell nobody."

CHAPTER 22

Mick tipped his hat at her before shutting the door behind him. He wasn't looking where he was going and walked right into the lady doctor.

"Ma'am, I am so sorry, I didn't watch where I was going."

"No harm was done, Mr. Quinn. Wilma asked me to check on one of the children is she inside?"

"Yes, she is but could I ask you something?"

He saw the shutters come down immediately but plunged ahead. "I was wondering, well I got a friend and well the thing is..." Mick's mouth went dry at the thought of what he was asking.

"Just say what you want, Mr. Quinn." Erin's tone wasn't overly friendly. He was tempted to forget it but Mollie needed her help.

"Mollie, she's one of the girls who works over the saloon." He hoped she would take the hint. The color flushing her cheeks suggested she had.

"Is she ill?" she asked.

"No."

"Then why would she want to see a doctor?"

"Thing is, there's some stuff that girls, I mean ladies don't want to discuss with a man. If you get my meaning."

Erin looked at him speculatively. He couldn't meet her gaze, he was too embarrassed. For some reason, her opinion of him mattered.

"This girl is a ... friend of yours.?"

"Yes. Please Doc, can you find a way to speak to her. I think she might be being hurt but she won't tell me nothing." He played with his hat as he spoke.

"I will do my best, Mr. Quinn."

"Thank you. Wilma knows her so she will tell you how best to see her. I don't think, well, it's not suitable for you to walk into the saloon. You being a lady and all." Mick knew he was speaking too much but her being so close was unnerving. She smelled so nice and she looked pretty.

"I am a doctor first."

Mick didn't reply. That might be the way she saw it but for most of the folks living here in Clover Springs, she was a lady first and foremost.

"Thanks, Doc."

He caught a hint of a smile at his acknowledgment of her status. He stood taller. What was wrong with him? He'd met plenty of women in his travels but hadn't met one who could get under his skin as she did.

He walked down the street toward the mill. He wondered if the Doc knew about Dickie. Not that the man would touch a respectable woman. Mrs. Hofmeister was respectable. Yeah, but she was foreign. Why did that matter? It shouldn't but it did.

* * *

ERIN LOOKED at his retreating back. What was it about the man that made her want to get to know him better? She hadn't been as attracted to anyone before. Not even… Her mind shut down refusing to go to that place of pain.

"Morning Doc, are you comin' in?" Wilma's voice interrupted her thoughts.

Erin entered the kitchen, taking off her shawl and hanging it over the back of a chair.

"You look tired Doc, you feeling all right?"

Erin smiled at the genuine concern on the older woman's face. "I am fine. But I am worried about you."

Wilma's face turned stony. "Nothing to be worried about. I is good and dandy."

"But you're not, are you? Don't lie to me, Wilma. I'm a doctor. I can see your ankles are swelling and you get short of breath."

"Don't know how I feel about you looking at my ankles. I never asked you to."

"Stop being cross, Wilma. You asked me to check on Ellen and the baby." Erin tried to placate the older woman. The last thing she needed was Wilma to get more stressed.

"That's 'cause I is worried about them. Miss Ellen, she don't eat more than a little fly. And baby Jake, he only an itty bitty little thing. He should be feeding better."

"You are absolutely right on both counts. Jake should be thriving and Ellen eating more. But I am positive both will get better with your help. But only if you are here to give it." Erin, although kind, knew she had to be firm.

Wilma sat down suddenly.

"What is wrong with me doc?" The fear in the older woman's eyes made Erin pause.

"You are going to be fine, Wilma." At the look of disbelief on the older woman's face, Erin took her hand. "Look at me. I said you will be fine. You need to take things a little slower that's all. You are trying to do more than most women in their twenties do."

"But I is dizzy doc and my feet, they sure do swell up."

"Both signs your heart is working harder than it should. You have to listen to your body, Wilma. First, you need to rest more."

"But there is just so much to do."

"I am going to speak to Father Molloy about engaging some help for the orphanage as well as a new teacher. You and Ellen need a break."

"They'll replace me if I can't do the job. I seen it all the time. I ain't got anywhere else to go Doc. Please."

Erin watched horrified as the old woman cried real tears using her apron to cover her face.

"Wilma, stop it now." Erin stood up and put her arms around the woman. "You have been the strong one in this town long enough. Nobody is going to let you go anywhere. You just need to slow down a little. Pass some chores onto Samuel Higgins or some of the older children. You are surrounded by people who love you. Every day I hear people talking about you. Please stop crying, you will feel worse."

Wilma sniffled a little. Erin retook her seat and waited for the older woman to compose herself.

"Sorry Doc, I don't know what came over me. I ain't usually a cry baby."

"You are the same as most women of your age. You realize you can't do as much as you used to. For some reason that makes you think you will not be wanted. I have seen it happen over and over again. I promise you Wilma, nobody in this town wants to be rid of you."

"Charlie Staunton mightn't agree?"

"Well, there might be one or two. Now, are you going to let me help you?"

"Yes, Doc." Wilma stood.

"What are you doing?"

"Making us a cup of coffee."

"Sit down, Wilma, and listen to me. You have got to take this seriously. I want you to sit down every hour for at least ten minutes with your feet up. Like this." Erin demonstrated the position she wanted Wilma to adopt. Just as she lifted her legs, the kitchen door opened and Mick Quinn walked back in.

"Sorry Wilma, I forgot to tell... I beg your pardon."

Erin fell off the chair onto the floor. Wilma started laughing and couldn't stop. Erin glared at Mick who looked as if he was trying not to laugh. He held out a hand to help her up.

"Don't you ever knock?" Angry at being seen in such an unladylike position she took her temper out on him.

"Actually I did knock but you two women were

talking so much, you didn't hear me." Mick looked at her. "Mind me asking what you were doing?"

"None of your business. Did you want something?" Erin knew she sounded rude but she didn't care. She just wanted him to leave, or else the ground to open and swallow her up. She was so embarrassed she could die.

"Gee I sure wish you could write up a tonic for that temper of yours. Wilma, I'll call in later when you don't have such unreasonable company."

Wilma was still laughing. A look from Erin only made her worse. Mick went out slamming the door behind him.

"That man!" Erin exclaimed.

"Yes, "Wilma agreed, before giving into more laughter.

"Wilma, if you don't stop I am leaving."

"Sorry, Doc, but you was ever so funny. Your face done turn bright red. But then you were flashing your underskirts at Mick."

"I didn't do that on purpose and you know it. Now, where was I?"

"You were trying to show me how to sit."

"I think you should lie on your bed and put your feet up on some pillows. That will help."

"I can't go to bed in the middle of the day. That ain't proper."

"Wilma, do you want my help?"

"Mick's right, you do need a tonic for that temper."

Erin was seething but she shouldn't take it out on a patient, particularly one as nice as Wilma. She kept her tone under control as she explained she wanted the older woman to rest more and eat less. "Your ankles will thank me if they have less weight to carry around."

"Here was me thinking you were a good addition to Clover Springs. Now I don't know what to think," Wilma muttered crossly.

"Is that a yes Doc Erin I will do what I am told?"

"Yes, Doc Erin," Wilma said before sticking her tongue out. Erin laughed. It was only seconds before Wilma joined in.

Ellen came into the room to find the two giggling like school girls.

"You two look like you are having a lot of fun."

"We is, Miss Ellen. How are you feeling?"

Erin noted Ellen's lack of color. She was sure the new mother was anemic.

"Ellen, I wanted to see you while I was here. I think it would be a good idea for you to feed Jake with goat's milk."

A mutinous expression clouded Ellen's face, "I want to feed him myself."

"I know you do and you are doing a great job. But

your illness during pregnancy has made you weak and Jake is a typical man. He's always hungry. If you try some goat's milk, you can ask Samuel to feed him at night allowing you to get more rest."

"Do you think it will help Jake? He isn't a very happy baby."

"He will be when his stomach is full."

"But I should be able to look after him properly. I'm not cut out to be a mother, am I?"

Before Erin could intervene, Wilma stood up and put her arms around Ellen. "Miss Ellen you be the best mother ever made. You are doing a fine job. Your baby is hungry that's all. Listen to Doc, she knows what she's talking about."

Erin wondered how much of her own advice would Wilma be willing to take.

"Ellen, you will see a huge difference in Jake, and you will feel much better too. Wilma, keep making her eat red meat. It helps the blood. I will call back in a few days to check my patients."

Wilma showed her to the door.

"All of them," Erin added just for the old lady's benefit. Wilma's lips tightened in acknowledgment.

* * *

As Erin walked back to the clinic, she was hoping she wouldn't bump into Mick again. But luck was against her.

"You look much better now Doc," he said grinning at her as she walked past.

She was tempted to stick her tongue out at him but that was childish. Instead, she stuck her nose in the air and walked past him. Any hopes her action had dented his pride was dashed as his laughter rang out loudly behind her.

CHAPTER 23

Erin stood outside the front door of the Red Feathers. Could she do this? She'd never been inside an establishment like it before. There was always a first time. She knocked at the door but there was no answer. She tried to open it but it was locked. Looking up, she caught one of the girls staring down at her.

"Can you please open the door?" Erin asked.

"Go away." The girl replied but not in a rude way. She seemed scared.

"My name is Doc Erin. I want to check you are all healthy."

"Go away please, Doc. He won't like it."

"Actually I don't care what he thinks. All I care about is you girls and the health of this town. The two matters are...interlinked." Erin took a deep breath. "Where is he?"

The girl didn't say anything but she glanced at the saloon. Erin had to take a deep breath. Going into a house full of soiled doves was one thing but a saloon? There would be lots of men in there and alcohol. And Mr. Dickinson. She had to speak to him.

She walked up to the door of the saloon. Speaking loudly, she addressed the inside of the saloon without actually stepping over the threshold.

"Mr. Dickinson, I wondered if I could have a word, please." Erin decided being polite might get her further.

There was no answer. She tried again.

"Mr. Dickinson, can you hear me?"

"The whole town can hear you, lady. What you want?" A surly looking barkeep peered out through the double doors.

"I would like to speak to the owner, Mr. Dickinson."

"Friend of yours?" The impertinent grin on the man's face was enough for Erin to lose her cool.

"No, he isn't. Excuse me." Using her medical bag as a buffer between them, she marched past the stunned barkeep.

It was much darker than she expected inside the saloon. Relieved to see there weren't that many men sitting around drinking, she looked around to find Mr. Dickinson. He was sitting at the table furthest from the door. She walked toward him. Two cowboys stood to bar her way.

"Excuse me, please."

"Go home lady, this ain't no place for you."

"I am not a lady. I am a doctor and I insist on speaking to Mr. Dickinson. Please excuse me."

She moved forward but they didn't move out of her way.

"What I have to say is of a private nature but if you wish me to discuss your boss's medical history over your arms, I shall do so. I don't think he will thank you for it though do you?" She peered into the face of one man. "Actually, you should consider calling into the clinic. That rash on your face could be a symptom of a rather unpleasant illness." She deliberately let her gaze travel over his body, hiding her amusement as his expression turned from cynical to fear.

A laugh from behind the men drew everyone's attention.

"You got spirit Doc. I like that in my female friends. Let her through, boys."

The men stood aside to let her pass. She could feel their eyes stripping her of her clothes, an experience she should be used to given the places she had doctored in before. But it was still unnerving. Without asking permission, she took a seat at the table. Leaning forward, she whispered none too quietly

"Mr. Dickinson I have reason to believe one or more of your girls are ill."

The conversation in the saloon had stopped the minute she entered. She knew they were all listening to her. Dickinson knew it too.

"Are you threatening me, lady?"

"Doc Erin is my name and no I am not. I am merely telling you of my suspicions. I would like to examine your... employees."

"Which one?"

Erin didn't hesitate. "All of them. The gentlemen I treated were a little vague on the name of the young ladies who ... entertained them."

Dickinson puffed on his cigar, the smoke blowing into her face. She didn't blink. She wasn't about to be intimidated.

"Let me be clear, Mr. Dickinson. I will examine each girl or I will stand outside the saloon and explain in some detail the symptoms of a certain disease. In particular, I will elaborate on the rather painful death your customers could anticipate."

Dickinson threw the cigar to the floor grounding it out with his foot.

"Enough. Nobody blackmails me, lady, not even a pretty doctor."

"I am not blackmailing you, sir. I am making you a promise." Intentionally she smiled and leaned in toward him as if she was flirting. In a low voice for his ears only, "It is your choice. Perhaps you don't know but I come from the Bronx in New York. I grew up surrounded by men just like you. You don't scare me, Mr. Dickinson. I will see those girls, one way or another."

His expression hardened as she met his gaze, not blinking. "Dusty, take the Doc over to the house. Stay with her when she talks to the girls."

Erin stood up. "Thank you for your understanding, Mr. Dickinson but Dusty will stay downstairs. My examination of the young ladies will be conducted in private. These are my terms."

She waited, her knees trembling. Had she pushed him too far? She matched him stare for stare all the time wondering if he had ever shown any emotion. The coldness in his expression almost made her run out the door. But she'd made a promise to check the girls. And she always kept her promises.

Dickinson took a step toward her, leaning forward as if to kiss her cheek. She pushed down her instinct to draw back, holding her back tall and straight.

"You won this time, lady, but don't ever push your luck with me again. You won't be so lucky next time," he whispered in her ear before drawing back.

She held out her hand to him challenging him to shake it. "Thank you for your co-operation, Mr. Dickinson. I look forward to seeing you often. I intend to make these checkups part of my regular routine." With a smile of triumph and a swish of her skirts, she turned her back on him and walked toward the exit.

“Come along Dusty, your boss won't want to pay for my time if I waste it waiting for you to catch up."

The customers in the saloon laughed as she walked past closely followed by Dusty.

CHAPTER 24

Still shaking from her encounter with Dickinson, Erin was relieved when Dusty opened the door of the Red Feathers without further comment. He walked in leaving her to follow him. Shutting the door behind her, she grimaced as Dusty yelled at the girls.

"Lady Doc is here to examine ya. Seems you be making people sick."

"I ain't sick. None of us are. What is she doing here?"

Dusty pushed the girl toward the Doc. Erin cringed at his rough treatment of the young girl. If that was the way he dealt with the girls when he had witnesses. What did they suffer when nobody was around.

A number of girls stood on different steps of the

staircase. Some were older and looked like seasoned workers but a couple stood out as being very young. Erin smiled at all of them.

"Good morning, ladies. My name is Doc Erin. I came to have a talk with you all. I am here to help and see what I can do to make your lives more...comfortable."

"We are doin' fine. We don't need no do-gooders in here. See ya." The girl looked at Dusty for approval but he wasn't paying attention.

Erin moved toward the staircase but Dusty moved quicker and stood in her way.

"Whatcha doing? You ain't going up there."

"Yes, I am. I have no intention of examining any lady downstairs."

"The boss won't like it."

"Well, I'm not going to tell him." Erin stared at him straight, recognizing him for the coward he was. "Dusty, the way I see it you got two choices. You can settle yourself down on that sofa over there and have a nap or you can go tell your boss the doctor is upstairs. Your choice. Now get out of my way, my time is too precious to stand here all day arguing."

Erin swept past him, making her way up the stairs. She smiled gently at a girl whose name she thought was Lily as she walked past her. "I really am here to help. I understand more than most what you girls are going through."

She could feel Lily staring at her but at least the girl didn't put up any more arguments. At the top of the stairs, she glimpsed a couple of luxury bedrooms as the doors were open. She knew the girls didn't live in those rooms. She was determined to see just how they lived. She made her way toward the one closed door only to find her route blocked by another scantily clad girl who looked terrified.

"You can't go in there. Nobody's allowed to see."

"Now ladies, we don't have much time. Mr. Dickinson wasn't keen on my visiting with you. I know you are suspicious and I don't blame you for that." Erin turned to speak directly to Lily who seemed to be the ring leader. "I know women like me don't treat you ladies with respect. I am not like that. I am a doctor and I want to help."

"What do you get out of it?"

"Lily, don't be rude. She may be telling the truth," a young girl spoke.

"Ain't nobody does nothing for free."

"Lily, I understand why you feel that way. I am not working for free. I intend to send my bill to Mr. Dickinson."

"You're going to get Dickie to pay you to take care

of us?" Lily said, disbelief fighting with admiration on her face.

"Yes, I am. Now, who is going to let me examine them first."

"I will."

"Mollie, you can't. You know Dickie won't be happy," Lily admonished her but Erin sensed she was coming around to the idea.

"Lily, why don't I start with you and you can then send in the other girls. You can explain there is nothing to be afraid of."

By challenging the girl's fear in front to the other girls, Lily had no choice but to submit to the examination. Lily led the way through the locked door with Erin and the other girls following in her wake. The rooms on this side couldn't have looked more different than the rooms at the front of the house. There were three or four cots in each room. The air was stagnant as the windows appeared to be nailed shut. Erin could see evidence of alcohol everywhere. No wonder really. If she had to live the life these girls did, she would probably drink too.

"Lily, perhaps you could sit down and I will start the examination."

Lily sat at the end of one of the cots.

"If you find something, do you have to tell Dickie?"

The fear in the girl's face made Erin's heartbreak.

"Our examination is private. Just you and me. Do you think something is wrong with you?"

Lily took a few seconds to answer. Erin sensed she was probably trying to decide could she trust her. "Lily I promise, nothing you tell me will be repeated."

Lily nodded before she inched up her skirt to reveal a nasty looking wound in her thigh. It had an angry red look.

"That looks very painful. Have you been cleaning it?"

"I washed it but it didn't help."

"I will show you what to do. First of all, you cannot touch it until you wash your hands thoroughly with soap and hot water." Erin asked one of the girls standing outside the room to get her a clean bowl of hot water. She looked in her bag and took out a small bottle. "If you put this on twice a day and cover it with a small bandage, it will heal in no time at all."

Erin reached into her bag and took out some squares of white material. "Cut these in two. Change the dressing twice a day. I will come back later in the week to check on you."

Erin gave the girl's hand a squeeze. "Please Lily, if you ever get hurt again like this, come and see me. Don't wait until it gets worse."

Lily didn't answer but gave a quick nod of her head.

"Do you girls have enough to eat? You are all very slim."

They were skin and bones but Erin didn't want to offend them.

"Dickie feeds us well enough. If we're good."

"He controls you by the use of food as well as violence?" At Lily's blank look, Erin explained."He hits you to make you behave?"

"Only when we deserve it. He ain't the worst."

Erin knew she wouldn't get any more out of Lily. She knew when she had pushed hard enough. She treated a succession of small wounds or bruises in each girl, all the while giving them instructions on how to look after themselves better. The last girl in to see her was Mollie.

"Lily, would you mind checking on Dusty while I see to Mollie. I don't want him going to get Dickie."

Erin wanted Mollie to speak freely and she didn't think the girl would do that with Lily hanging around. She was right. As soon as Lily was out of the way, Mollie started talking and didn't stop.

"You got to see to Kathryn. She is real sick."

"I've seen everyone. You all have a lot of minor injuries but nobody is very ill. " Erin tried to reassure the young girl.

"You ain't seen, Kathryn. They got her hidden

downstairs out in the back room. None of us is allowed to go near her. Except for Lily."

"Why? What's wrong with her?"

"She got beat up real bad. She was screaming but he didn't do nothing to stop it. He don't care so long as gets his money. She was nice to me. She had a lovely smile."

Erin assumed He was Dickinson. She didn't like the way Mollie was speaking about the girl in the past tense. She couldn't have died and her body hidden. Could she?

"Let me examine you first Mollie and then I will ask Lily about Kathryn."

"You can't ask her. She'll know it was me. You got to come back and find her."

Mollie was so agitated, Erin agreed. She didn't want to do anything to put the young girl in danger.

"Mollie, what age are you?"

"Don't know," Mollie replied.

"Please don't lie to me," Erin said softly.

"Fourteen."

"How long have you been with Dickie?"

"Three months. " Mollie picked at her nails. "He seemed nice. I was hungry and scared. He brought me some food and some clothes. Said he was going to look after me. He did at the start. Then he brought me here."

Erin wanted to hug the girl but knew it would not be welcome.

"Mollie, a friend of yours asked me to look after you."

"Mick." The hope shining out of her eyes made Erin wish she hadn't said anything.

"If you need me, you come to find me. Anytime."

"Doc, do you think Mick will be able to get me out of here? I don't know how much longer I can stand it."

Erin took the girls hand in hers. "I know he will do his best. We all will. Now I best go or Mr. Dickinson will come and look for me. Try to get more to eat Mollie."

Erin stood up. She called Lily and the other girls.

"I am going to go back to Mr. Dickinson now and demand he open these windows. You need extra light and fresh air. This place is a fire hazard. If there was a fire downstairs you wouldn't get out. I will also insist on hot water for baths and more food. Is there anything else you would like me to get for you?"

"A coat?" One of the girls asked. "If we have to go to the store, I feel funny wearing the clothes we have. Everyone stares at us."

Erin smiled. "I will get you some coats. Now you all know where the clinic is. If you ever need my help, you come to find me."

Erin looked at each face individually. The majority

of the girls wouldn't make eye contact. Life was probably never going to improve for them. But Lily and Mollie did. They were two of a kind despite the age difference. Both survivors.

* * *

ERIN WALKED BACK DOWNSTAIRS. Pulling on her gloves, she gave Dusty's leg a sharp kick to wake him up.

"I have to speak to Mr. Dickinson. Tell him I will wait for him outside. I need some clean air."

"He ain't going to like that. He'll expect you to go to him."

"I am not his lackey. Unless he wants me to go direct to the sheriff, he will meet me outside. Good day."

Erin walked out the door leaving Dusty cursing her. She allowed herself a small smile. She had a mountain of work to do before she really helped the girls living in the house but at least she had won the first battle.

Dickie kept her waiting for some time before making his way outside.

"Thought you would have gone home, Doc."

"I never give up Mr. Dickinson. Now about those girls, these are my..."

"I don't intend doing any different so you might as

well save yourself and me the trouble. Good afternoon Miss Brennan."

Erin ignored the slight. She looked at him saying, "That truly is a pity, Mr. Dickinson, as my next stop is the sheriff's office. Those locked windows are a fire hazard. Having windows nailed shut in a building used for public entertainment is in breach of the Fire Safety regulations, subsection ten. You can be fined up to 100 dollars for each breach of the code. Have a nice day."

"Wait a minute. I ain't never heard of no code."

"Didn't I tell you my pa was a fire chief back in New York?'

"Okay lady you win. This time."

"While you are unlocking those windows, it would be a good idea to provide new bedding, plenty of hot water and clean cloths. I am sure the girls won't mind cleaning up the squalor they call home. I expect you to place an order at the store for more food too. Next time I examine your workers, I would prefer to see some meat on their bones."

"Don't push your luck lady."

"It's Doctor, not lady. Good afternoon, Mr. Dickinson."

Erin walked down the street with a big smile on her face. She hated bullies of all descriptions and getting the upper hand on one always made her day.

* * *

SOMETIME LATER THE clinic door opened, admitting Little Beaver.

"Afternoon Doc, you got a minute?"

"Yes of course. Are you hurt?" Erin scanned him but didn't see any sign of injury. He looked much healthier than most of the townsfolk.

"I have had a complaint Doc. Sheriff sent me to talk to you about it."

"A complaint?"Erin racked her brains but couldn't think of anyone who would have reason to complain to the sheriff.

"Seems like you been threatening a businessman." Little Beaver grinned at her.

"He made a complaint?" Erin stood up. "Of all the low down skunks."

"You do have a very hot temper. Yes, Mr. Dickinson is very upset. He says we must punish you for breaking the law."

"What law?"

"He didn't know." Little Beaver started to laugh. "He jump up and down a lot. He looked like he was trying to do a war dance but was drunk."

Erin giggled at the description.

"Little Beaver, I am glad you called. I need your help."

Erin quickly told the Indian the story Mollie told her. "I have no idea where this Kathryn is now or even if she is still alive. Can you do anything?"

"I can search the building later. "

"Don't you need some papers?"

"Only if I get caught." Little Beaver winked at Erin.

"Be careful. Please call me if I can do anything to help you."

Little Beaver's face turned serious.

"Doc Erin, you need be more careful. Mr. Dickinson is angry. He like snake. Never turn your back on snake."

"I will be careful."

"You must or Mick will be very bad to Little Beaver."

Little Beaver left Erin wondering what Mick had to do with her. Surely the Indian wasn't trying to play matchmaker?

* * *

EARLY THE NEXT MORNING, Little Beaver called to see Erin at the clinic. He told her he had searched the building but couldn't find Kathryn. "There was blood stains but I cannot say if human or animal."

Erin looked him in the eyes. She didn't say

anything. Neither did he but he touched her arm gently. Then he moved to the door.

"One day soon, we will stop this man from hurting anyone else. This I promise."

"Thank you," she whispered, the lump in her throat making her unable to talk properly.

CHAPTER 25

Erin was reading an old copy of the New England Journal of Medicine. The clinic was so clean you could eat your dinner off the floor. The shelves were tidy, the accounts up to date. She had even packed her bag ready for her trip up to the logging village. Mrs. Grey had thrown an almighty fit when Erin suggested she was considering going up there alone. She insisted on finding her a male escort. If truth be known her tales of grizzly bears, mountain lions, and the odd fugitive had scared Erin not that she would admit it.

She looked up as the clinic door opened. Mick stood on the doorstep. Without even thinking, she quickly checked her reflection in the mirror. She hadn't seen him since her unfortunate display in

Wilma's kitchen. Judging by the merry gleam in his eyes, he hadn't forgotten how embarrassed she'd been. She would have to pretend it never happened. Adopting her most professional manner, she closed the periodical and replaced it on Doc's desk.

"Morning Doc, are you ready to go?"

"Sorry, Mr. Quinn but I am not following. Go where?"

"Davy said you needed an escort up to the logging camp on the peak."

"Mrs. Grey said she'd ask him for someone. I wasn't expecting you. I will ask -"

'There's nobody else. They all got jobs to do. So are you going or not?"

Erin longed to say no but she couldn't. Doc said he hadn't been up to the village in a long time. The loggers tended to fend for themselves. She wanted to check everyone was as healthy as could be. Come winter it would be impossible to reach them.

"I'm ready."

"You need to wrap up warmer than that. It might look like a nice day but it will be cold up there."

Erin wasn't about to argue. She ran upstairs and brought down a blanket. "Happy now?"

He didn't answer but held out his hand to help her up into the wagon beside him.

"We will go as far as we can in this but we may have to walk some of the way."

"I have sturdy boots, Pa!" She said trying to make a joke. She thought she caught the hint of a smile but he turned away before she was certain. It was going to be a long trip. She settled back and decided to try and sleep.

* * *

IT DIDN'T TAKE AS LONG as she'd thought. The loggers were up higher in the mountain working but their wives and children were camping on lower ground. Mick spent his time playing games with the younger children while Erin chatted with the mothers as best she could. One of the women knew some English and between that and sign language they muddled along. She was happy with the overall health of the majority of the children. They looked cleaner than she'd expected too. She was about to leave when she heard the frail cries of an infant. She moved toward the sound to find a woman lying in her house, the baby lying beside her.

"Why is she left alone like this?" Erin asked. The house was in a complete state of squalor. The bed was unmade, the baby and mother were both dirty.

"Husband leave her. She bad woman."

The woman who had been acting as interpreter went to leave.

"Wait. You can't leave her like this. She will die."

"Best for all if she did."

"But her child? He or she is completely innocent," Erin said.

"Child of sin. Best if she die too."

The woman walked out the door leaving Erin staring speechless after her. If she hadn't seen the same woman being so kind to the children outside, she wouldn't have been as surprised. She quickly made her way toward the baby and mother.

"My name is Doc Erin. I will help you."

If the woman understood her, she made no sign of it. She just stared.

Erin picked up the baby, disgusted to find the poor thing was completely saturated.

"Mr. Quinn, can you help me here, please."

Mick looked surprised to be called but he came over right away. He took one look at the baby and his expression turned so angry, Erin took a step back.

"What do you need doc?" he asked through gritted teeth.

"Can you speak their language? I don't know if she understands English. The other woman, Maria, won't help me."

Mick tried speaking to the mother. She was

surprised to see how gentle he was. He took the lady's hand and stroked it gently. She talked rapidly at first but he made her understand she had to speak more slowly.

"Can you ask her when she gave birth?" Erin asked.

"Two days ago. She thinks. She isn't sure."

"Did anyone help her?"

"No." Mick's teeth gritted.

"We need to find some food for the baby and get them both washed. Do any of the children you were playing with speak English? I need plenty of hot water, fuel for the fire and a nurse."

"The water and the wood I can do. A nurse? Out here?"

"A new mother who is feeding her baby," Erin explained slightly amused as his face went red.

"Oh. As for the children, a few go to school occasionally. I will go get one of the older girls."

A girl called Olga came into the hut, a scared expression on her face. "Matuska not want me in here."

"Let me deal with your ma. I need your help. Have any of the women given birth recently?" Erin asked.

"Ya, two."

"Are they still feeding their babies?" Erin mimed out in actions so the girl understood. Mick made himself busy bringing in fuel.

Olga nodded.

"Can you ask them to come here please?" Erin asked.

"To this house. Nobody comes here." Olga shook her head vigorously.

"Tell them the doctor said to come."

Olga went to find the women. Meanwhile, Erin busied herself washing the little girl. She was such a tiny little thing, already listless. Whatever fight she'd left seemed to have been used up by wailing earlier. Erin sponged her down gently trying to keep a grip on the rage building inside her at the condition of the infant's skin.

The two nursing mothers arrived.

"Can you please feed this child?" Erin again mimed out the actions.

"Nah." The women went to leave but Erin stopped them.

"The child will die if you don't." Erin gestured to Olga to translate. The younger girl spoke rapidly but the women kept walking.

"I will never come back to this village again. I will make sure the other doctor doesn't either. Do you hear me?" The women didn't answer her. "I mean it."

"Shouting at people rarely works," Mick said out of the side of his mouth. Why don't you try asking them?"

Erin wanted to snap his head off but instead, she took a deep breath and looked directly into the ladies' faces.

"Please. I do not understand what the mother has done but this is just a little girl."

Olga translated again. One woman left but the other looked at the baby. Taking a big sigh, she took the child from Erin. Settling herself back on a chair she started nursing her. The infant was slow to suckle but after a couple of attempts, she began gulping in the milk. Both Erin and the nursing mother laughed. Olga had disappeared.

A weak sound from the bed alerted her to the fact the mother was crying.

"Please take my baby. Do not leave here to die." The mother grasped Erin's arm. Although weak, her nails dug into Erin's skin.

"You will be able to look after her yourself. A couple of days rest and you will be fine," Erin said, preparing some cloths to wash the woman. Then she would sort out the rest of the house. The woman didn't respond but lay on the bed with her eyes closed.

"Doc, you might want to..."

'Thank you for your advice earlier but I know what I am doing," She snapped back. She wasn't angry with him but totally overwhelmed at the situation they were in. Mick threw his eyes up to heaven before retreating toward the door.

Erin pulled back the bedcovers only to realize the women wasn't sleeping but had died. Horrified she looked up at Mick who was staring at her with a mixture of pity and I told you so look.

"Probably best for her sake," he offered.

"How can you say that. Her daughter needs her." She was fighting back tears of frustration.

"Erin, you don't know these people. You saw how hard it was to get help for the baby. There is no way they would have helped the mother." His tone was gentle but firm.

"But why? What could she have done that was so bad she was more or less banished?"

"Her husband says the baby is not his."

The nursing mother said without looking at either of them. Erin was surprised to find she understood English.

"But why?"

The mother shrugged. "They have been married many years and no babies. Then he goes away for six months, comes back and she is pregnant. At first, he is happy. But then the men start talking, women say things. He beats her and she confessed. The baby, not his."

Erin couldn't hold back her tears, the poor dead girl only looked to be about twenty.

"But where would she meet another man up here?"

"She didn't but nobody believed her."

"You did. Why didn't you help her?" Erin asked.

"Me? My husband would have beat me too. You do not know what it is like. Our ways are different. My husband would not do women's work like your one is."

"My husband?"

Erin realized the woman was talking about Mick. He had boiled lots of water and set and lit the fire. He grinned over at her obviously amused by her embarrassment. She didn't know where to look.

"Will the father want the baby now his wife is dead?' she asked.

The nursing mother shook her head sadly.

"He sent letter to his parents asking them to find a new wife. She will not want this child."

"So what will happen to her?"

The nursing woman met Erin's eyes. "You do not want to know the answer."

Erin's stomach heaved. Holding a hand to her mouth, she made it out the door just in time. Mick waited behind her until she was finished before handing her a small cloth.

"It's not the cleanest but it's the best I could find."

"Thank you," she whispered, wiping her mouth. He put a hand on her shoulder, and, for a second, she was tempted to turn around. He might put his arms around her. Flustered by feeling weak, she muttered. "I have to get out of here. I don't know how they can live with themselves."

"It's a hard life being a logger and having a family. These people have very little. Can't really blame them for not wanting to take in a child of strangers."

"I am taking the child. I am not leaving it here to, to…" Erin couldn't say the word. She turned her back and marched into the cabin. She rummaged through the box at the bottom of the bed. As she suspected, she found some small baby clothes. Her heart ached for the young mother who had obviously been excited to find out she was finally pregnant.

"I will care for your daughter. I promise." Erin said as she set about laying the young mother out. Mick dug a grave with the help of some of the older boys. They carried the body to the grave, said a quick prayer and taking the baby with them left the camp before the men got back.

"Please tell the father I have the baby. He can come into Clover Springs to collect her if he wishes." Erin asked the nursing mother.

"I will tell but he won't be down."

Erin saw the woman believed what she was saying.

Still, she hoped that when the man realized his young wife was dead and child missing, he would see more clearly.

* * *

ERIN CUDDLED the baby as they made their way back down to Clover Springs. Mick was quiet for which she was grateful. She couldn't believe so much had happened in the twelve or so hours since they had left that morning.

"Don't be too harsh on them," Mick said after they had put some distance between them and the logging camp. "It's a hard life and not everyone has what it takes."

"To do what? Look out for another human being. Whatever the truth about the mother or father, this baby is innocent. Why should she suffer?"

"Erin, be realistic. There are some things you can't change. Aaron filled me in on the orphans his wife helped Father Molloy rescue on the train. There were thirty children traveling to goodness knows what end on that train. You can't rescue all of them."

"You say that yet I know what you have been doing in town."

* * *

Did she know about Mollie? How could that have happened? Nobody but Cookie and Wilma were aware of what was going on there.

"You have gone quiet now. Mrs. Sullivan told me you are the first to help those in trouble. The widow's friend is what she called you."

Mick bristled. That nickname could have a totally different meaning.

"I just help where I can, same as anyone else."

"But don't you see Mick, it's not the same. Those people up there probably grew up with the girl who died yet they wouldn't help her baby."

"The nursing mother did."

"Only because we bribed her into it. How can people be so cruel?"

It dawned on him she wasn't just talking about today. He wasn't sure what had happened in her past but something similar. Maybe she had lost a child? Not a question you could ask a single lady though. She might turf him out of the wagon just for even thinking it.

"What else has Martha Sullivan been saying about me then?" he asked.

"Not a lot." She turned a lovely shade of pink.

"That's a mighty pretty color on you, Doc."

"This old dress?"

"No, the pink in your cheeks."

He grinned as she blushed deeper.

"You are teasing me, Mr. Quinn."

"That I am but what happened to Mick. You have been calling me Mick all day. I like it." He liked it a lot but he wasn't about to admit that. His feelings about the doc bothered him. Sometimes he was fit to strangle her and other times he wanted to pull her into his arms and kiss her until she was breathless.

"It's not proper. People will talk."

Mick laughed and earned himself a dirty look in the process. "Listen, Doc, for all your intelligence you don't always use the brain you've got. People around here talk. They ain't got much else to do. Life is fairly boring when you do the same thing day in, day out. Gossiping helps pass the time."

He wasn't prepared for the look of abject fear on her face.

"But they don't know anything about me?"

What did she have to hide? Something had her rattled. He sought to reassure her.

"They don't need to. They'll just make it up. The fact we took a trip together and have been gone for hours is bound to be discussed the length and breadth of Clover Springs tonight."

"Oh!"

"You're not used to living somewhere so small are

you? What made you leave New York if you don't mind me asking?"

"Big cities can become too small sometimes. The number of immigrants is pushing the city to its limits. There are problems everywhere. I couldn't do anything so I left for somewhere I could use my skills better."

Her reply sounded like a well-practiced excuse rather than a real reason, but he sensed it was all the information he would get. At least for now.

"And that's Clover Springs?" he asked, despite himself.

"For now it is. I don't know what the future will bring."

The baby started to wail.

"What you going to feed it on now? Apart from Ellen, I don't think we have any women in Clover Springs who just gave birth."

Erin rocked the baby trying to soothe her, "Ellen is too weak to help. But we have some goats. She will have to get used to that. Do you think Wilma will take her at the orphanage?"

"I thought you planned on keeping her?"

"Me? What would I do with a baby? I can't exactly bring her out visiting patients. Anyway, it's better she had a mother and a father."

She sounded like she was trying to convince herself the baby was better with someone else.

"Ah, you are traditional after all?"

"I am not sure what that means, Mr. Quinn."

Mick knew when to shut up. Calling him Mr. Quinn was her way of setting a distance between them. Suited him just fine as he wasn't getting involved with anyone, especially not a female doctor who was stubborn as a mule.

CHAPTER 26

Mick stopped at the orphanage on the way back. He carried Doc's bags while Erin carried the baby.

As soon as they entered the kitchen, Wilma reached for the child.

"Oh isn't she tiny? What's her name?"

Erin blushed. She'd forgotten to ask the mother's name never mind whether she had thought of one for the baby.

"I've no idea. I forgot to ask," Erin quickly told Wilma and Ellen what had happened up at the camp.

"Poor little tyke. Imagine being born and allowed to die. Good job you was there, Doc. Sounds like you were meant to be."

Erin couldn't bear to think of how close she had

got to leaving. If the baby hadn't cried out, she wouldn't have known anything about her.

"Why don't you call her Erin?" Wilma asked.

Erin shook her head. "No, I couldn't do that. It doesn't feel right."

"What about Michelle? You know in honor of Mick helping to rescue her," Ellen added.

"I think that's lovely, Ellen. What do you think, Doc?"

Erin took the baby back, holding her close. "I think it's a wonderful idea. Michelle suits her just fine."

She noticed Mick leaving quietly but not before she saw the look of pleasure on his face. He wasn't as immune to the baby as he pretended.

Erin rocked the little one who seemed content to sleep in her arms. It had taken a little while to get her to take the goats milk but when nothing better was available, she gave in. She was a survivor.

"Do you think you will be able to find parents for her, Wilma?"

"I reckon so. Most people want to adopt a baby as then they can rear it according to their ways. An older child is more difficult in lots of ways."

"Unless you are looking for someone to take on all your chores," Ellen said bitterly.

Erin was surprised at the bitter note in Ellen's

voice. From what little she knew of the school teacher, it wasn't in her nature to be nasty.

"Excuse me, Doc. Lack of sleep is making me cross. Alicia Higgins had to stop Charlie Staunton, he's the man who didn't want a female doc, from adopting two boys. He didn't want sons but extra cheap hands on his farm," Ellen explained.

"How awful. I am glad your friend was able to stop them."

"Why don't you come and visit Alicia with me tomorrow?" Wilma asked, "You two should get on like a house on fire. She's educated like you and comes from a big city." Wilma leaned in to take the baby back. "We could take this little one with us if you like."

"Sounds lovely. Thank you, Wilma. I best get back to the boarding house. Goodnight, ladies."

Erin left the orphanage quickly. She knew she was becoming too attached to Michelle. She had to maintain a professional distance. In her profession, she was bound to come across numerous waifs and strays. She couldn't adopt all of them. She'd wanted a baby for so long. Well, that wasn't going to happen now so she might as well close that door.

She was so engrossed in her thoughts, she didn't see the man in front of her before it was too late.

"I am so sorry, please forgive me." Erin looked up,

her stomach churning when she saw it was Mr. Dickinson from the Red Feathers.

"Nothing to forgive Miss..."

"Doctor Brennan." He knew who she was. "I was too busy thinking and not looking where I was going."

"No harm was done, Doc, but I kind of wish there was. Not every day you get to bump into a pretty lady doctor."

Before she could respond he held out his arm. "Please allow me to escort you home."

"Thank you but it isn't necessary."

"Well, Doc, don't you have a duty to check I am not hurt badly after you injured me."

Despite her detesting him, Erin laughed. "You said you weren't hurt."

"I lied. You owe me, Doc." He bowed and held out his arm once more.

What harm could it do to allow him to walk her to the boarding house?

Erin kept silent even though there were questions she wanted to ask. How could he sleep at night given the number of lives he had ruined. She was relieved when they arrived at the boarding house. She didn't want any arguments with him so thought she should be polite.

"Thank you very much, Mr. Dickinson, for the

escort and the company. It's been a long day. I really must retire. Goodnight," she said firmly.

"Goodnight Doc. See you again."

Erin stepped into the boarding house, closing the door behind her. She stood trying to calm her breathing. She could understand why girls like Mollie had fallen into Dickenson's clutches. He could be very charming when he wanted to be.

* * *

MICK HID IN THE SHADOWS, teeth clenched watching as Dickinson escorted Erin to the boarding house. Her tinkling laugh grated on his nerves. What on earth could she find to laugh about with that moppet on her arm? He wanted to jump out and drag her away from him. Why? She isn't your woman. No, but he is dangerous and she needs protecting. The voice inside his head kept arguing. He was glad he had waited to see her. He wanted to make sure she was all right after the emotional upheaval at the camp.

He watched her close the door leaving Dickinson standing outside. At least she was sensible. Still, the fact Dickie had sought out her company was worrisome. That man had an agenda for every action. What was he up to?

"You look troubled my friend."

Mick nearly jumped out of his own skin. He hadn't seen or heard Little Beaver approach him. The Indian laughed.

"You are not alone. I can do this with most people. The white man spends too much time talking and not listening."

Mick smiled. It was true.

"What are you looking at? Your face was fierce."

"Dickinson. I don't trust him."

"There is nothing new about that. I think the fact he had a hand on the doctor was a problem, no?"

"That oily snake should keep his hands to himself," Mick said. He was rewarded by laughter. He glared at Little Beaver but the Indian continued to laugh.

"Don't you have sheriff business to attend to?" he said.

Little Beaver kept laughing as he continued his patrol.

CHAPTER 27

The ladies had gathered for another sewing bee at Mary's house. Erin admired the Sullivan ranch. The house was beautiful but the view of the surrounding mountains and land took her breath away.

"Real pretty, ain't it?"

The hairs on the back of her neck rose at his voice. She had hoped she would see him. She had taken more care with her appearance telling herself she was doing so as she was meeting the other ladies.

"If I lived here, I don't think I would ever leave. It's so wild yet peaceful." She laughed self-consciously. "Listen to me. A city girl born and bred admiring a ranch."

"Everything you said was true but don't let the idyllic picture fool you. It can be really dangerous out here for those who aren't aware of the hidden dangers."

She glanced at him, suddenly thinking he wasn't just talking about their surroundings. She thought she saw admiration mixed with something else in his eyes. Was it hesitation or ... She blinked. Regardless of what was on his mind, she had no intention of ever being tied to a man.

"I am sure there are, Mr. Quinn but no doubt I will learn enough to survive the longer I spend here."

She saw the hint of a challenge in his eyes but before he could say anything further, she turned toward the ranch. "I best go inside. The ladies will be wondering what's keeping me."

* * *

"Doc Erin, would you come up to the goldmine with me? I am a bit concerned that the doctor employed by the previous owner is rather inept."

"I would love to. The mountain air would do me the world of good. When are you leaving?"

"You ladies can't just venture off into the mountains on your own," Wilma protested.

"Why not, you are always saying a woman can do a job as good as a man."

"Alicia, you know that ain't the truth. I never said

stuff like that. I said a woman is often just as clever as a man but sometimes you need a man around. Can you fire a gun, Erin?"

"No. There wasn't much call for that in New York."

"See! What happens if you meet some nasty men up there in the woods?" Wilma's agitated tone warned them her temper was rising. "You got to take the men and that's final."

"Aaron can't spare any more time from the homestead. Anyway, he gets in the way. He won't let me have a real look at what's going on."

"You mean he tryin' to keep you safe. He done tole me about you trying to go down into the mines. What you thinking of girl, you ain't no miner. You a mother now. Harry and Steven have been through enough without having to lose another mama."

"Wilma, please calm down. I told you to rest more," Erin admonished.

Alicia rounded on Wilma. "Why have you to rest? Have you been sick and not told me?"

"Thanks, Doc!" Wilma's sarcastic reply made Erin wince. She shouldn't have mentioned Wilma's health in front of Alicia. It wasn't professional but the older woman needed to take things easier. She needed to lose some weight too. Neither opinion had sat well with Wilma.

"I told Wilma she is at an age in life where she

should be taking things more slowly. That's all," Erin quickly reassured Alicia. "Now who could escort us to the mine?"

"Who's going to the mine?" Samuel walked into the kitchen followed by Little Beaver. "Little Beaver is hungry, Ma. Got any cookies you can spare him?"

"Don't you try your tricks on your ma, Mr. Samuel. Ellen done tole me not to let you eat so much."

Mrs. Higgins laughed at the exchange between her son and Wilma. "Wilma is like another ma to my Samuel," she said to Erin who smiled back at her.

"What Ellen doesn't know won't hurt her," Samuel replied cheekily as he quickly grabbed two cookies. "So who is going to the mine?"

"I asked Doc Erin to check on my miners before the heavy winter sets in. I am worried about them. The current doctor, who had been there since the old manager, doesn't do much apart from prescribing his tonic. It cures everything from measles to hangovers from what I can work out."

"I will go with you. I have to check for men making moon liquid Many men were sick from drinking at the saloon. Says its bad whiskey," Little Beaver said before taking another cookie.

"Moon liquid? Oh, you mean moonshine. They make that in Ireland, too, from potatoes. It's called poteen. It smells disgusting but unfortunately, people still drink it. It's very dangerous and illegal in Ireland. I didn't know it was against the law to make it here."

"It is not. They can make it all they like to drink themselves. But the men at the saloon shouldn't be getting sick. Sheriff wants them moved on." Little Beaver kept taking cookies.

"Quite right too. There is enough illness without having to deal with self-induced hangovers," Alicia said.

"This is a bit more dangerous than hangovers Alicia," Erin replied, "Bad whiskey can quickly kill a man."

"Who else you taking with you Little Beaver? I wish I could come but my leg isn't up to it," Samuel asked.

"I will ask Mick and a couple of other men to come. Cookie too. He is good to have on the trail."

"Cookie?" Erin asked rather mystified.

"I don't know his real name. He is a friend of Mick Quinn's. Stays on the Sullivan ranch sometimes. He can shoot straighter than most anyone I know. His cooking ain't bad for a man." Samuel reached for another cookie but this time his ma lightly hit his hand away.

Erin couldn't help the twinge of excitement at the thought of spending time with Mick again. She was amazed by how easy she found it to talk to him. Was his concern for Mollie friendly or romantic? She didn't want to think about how that made her feel.

"I will go ask Davy if he can spare the men. I can deputize Mick and Cookie as the sheriff is concerned we have a number of camps set up in the foothills of the mountains."

"We got enough problems here with that Red house. We don't need no mountain juice on top of it. Men drink that and then the fighting starts. My babies don't need to watch gunfights."

Everyone smiled at Wilma's description of the orphans. It could apply to any child in Clover Springs. As far as Wilma was concerned they were all her babies.

CHAPTER 28

"I don't know how these women live all the way up here. It's so remote isn't it?" Alicia said to Erin. "But I guess you think our homestead is remote after living in New York. In the City, there are people everywhere."

"I think your homestead is lovely. I don't miss New York with the smells, the lack of sanitation and the overcrowding. You should see how some of the people live. In tenement buildings, two or more families live in a space hardly big enough for a couple." Erin looked at the view around her. "I know it's a tough life out here but I wonder which is worse?"

"I want you to tell me what improvements you think we could make for the people working in the mine. Not inside it," Alicia hastened to add. "I mean the houses and things. I want the people to be happy."

"I heard engaging a good cook keeps the workers happy," Erin replied with a smile.

"You think that's a joke. So did I until I heard of men departing one mine for another simply because the cook kept burning the food. A lot of the men's wives have moved up here so they take care of a lot of the cooking. Some single men give them a few coins in return for cooking and laundry. Others prefer to eat in the main tent. They leave their laundry longer too." Alicia's nose wrinkled, no doubt remembering the smell from her previous visit.

* * *

THEY SOON ARRIVED at the camp. A group of disheveled looking children came down to greet them. Erin was dismayed to see a few showed signs of scurvy. What she couldn't understand was why? There were plenty of fruits available in the mountains. She moved slowly into the camp wondering what other issues she would find.

The women greeted Alicia like a long lost friend. Erin watched the smiles as they chattered with her new friend all trying to talk at once. Little Beaver and his men stayed only for a cup of coffee before they ventured higher in the direction of the mine itself. Erin wanted to go with them. She had never seen a mining operation before but they said it was too dangerous. Anyway, she had a job to do. As soon as the women knew she was a doctor, they lined up patients to see her including to her dismay a rather ornery goat.

"Can't they understand I am not a veterinarian?"

“They don’t know what that is. If you can cure people you can cure this old goat." Alicia tried her best to hide her giggles but Erin knew she was amused.

"Not sure I can, I have no idea what is wrong with it apart from it being severely cranky." Erin resolved to leave the goat to last preferring to deal with her human patients first. Quite a few of the children were complaining about belly ache. She quickly established they were constipated. Their mothers were turning the precious cow milk into butter and leaving them to drink the remnants. Erin patiently explained the process of churning took all the goodness out of the milk. Growing children needed to drink a full glass of milk for breakfast and in the evening. At the dismayed looks around the campfire, Erin suspected they couldn’t afford to keep more cows. Alicia immediately offered to send some goats up to the camp. They would adapt better to mountain life and their milk was good for the children.

Erin explained more about nutrition emphasizing the need to keep the children warm particularly in the winter months. She tried to convince the women they should move further down the mountain as they weren't acclimatized to the Colorado weather but they refused. They wanted to be near their men. She suggested to Alicia they consider building log cabins for the families to live in rather than the lean-to's they currently occupied.

* * *

ON VISITING THE LEAN-TOS, she was pleased to see most of them were kept as clean as possible. She gave them all lectures on the importance of washing their hands before eating or dressing any wounds. Although they were already storing meat for the winter, they didn't seem to see that a balanced diet was vital for survival. She advised them to can as much fruit and vegetables as they could to help prevent scurvy. Increasing the number of potatoes they ate would also help. Last but not least, she advised them on the best locations for their privies. She didn't want them to set up an outhouse too near to their source of running water. Thankfully, there were no arguments on that score.

The ladies prepared a feast of mashed potatoes, roast pork and stewed tomatoes for dinner followed by some kind of pie. Erin wasn't sure what it was but it tasted delicious. The men had yet to come back from their travels so Alicia and Erin gratefully accepted the offer of a bed for the night.

* * *

THE NEXT MORNING they breakfasted on flapjacks and cackleberries. "Why do they call eggs cackleberries?"

"I have no idea, Erin. Sometimes I think we speak a different language in the East don't you?"

Erin was so glad Alicia had come from Boston and settled in Clover Springs. While she loved her new town, it was nice to have someone who understood the differences in lifestyle.

A commotion in the forest alerted the camp.

"Doc, we need you. One of the loggers got hit by a widow maker. He's hurt bad."

"A widow-maker?" Erin turned to ask Alicia but she shrugged her shoulders. A miner's wife clarified that when the loggers cut down the trees, sometimes they fell on the men by mistake.

Erin washed her hands carefully in the boiled water some women had set aside for laundry. Then she picked up her bag and headed back into the mountain with the men. Alicia trailed after her.

The loggers camp was as different from the women's

camp as one could find. Erin only saw one woman and a couple of children. The rest of the place swarmed with bearded giants speaking a foreign language.

"Most of the men are from Norway and Sweden. Many don't bring their families with them. The work is too dangerous. They could be killed and leave their families destitute in a foreign country," Alicia explained.

"Alicia, I need somewhere to work. Do any of these people speak English?"

"Ja, missy, I do. What you need?" Erin looked up to see the tallest broadest man she had ever seen smiling down at her, his eyes full of concern.

"I need a tent and lots of boiling water. And some clean cloths." The man called out orders in his native tongue. People ran to do his bidding. Meanwhile, some men arrived back in camp carrying the patient.

The giant showed them to a hastily emptied tent. The injured man was still conscious, his pale pinched face half covered by a thick bushy beard. His arm was wrapped in a blood-soaked shirt. Erin was glad to see it seemed to be clean. She unwrapped the makeshift bandage as gently as she could. The man gritted his teeth but didn't cry out despite the considerable pain he must have been in.

"My name is Doc Erin. I will do my best to help

you but I'm afraid I don't have anything to give you for the pain."

She didn't know if the man understood her but the giant whose name was Erik translated for him anyway. The patient murmured something. Erin looked at Erik.

"Karl says it's okay someone gave him lots of whiskeys."

"I really wish they hadn't. You best keep an eye on him. He is likely to vomit everywhere." She examined Karl carefully to ensure he didn't have a fever and wasn't losing too much blood. "Mick, could you please put a log under his feet so they are higher than his head."

"Yes, ma'am."

"Is Little Beaver with you?"

"No, ma'am. We split up and he hasn't come back yet."

"I will need some men with strong stomachs to help me. I am going to have to set his arm and it is better if he doesn't move while I am doing it. He will need to be held down."

"I will help with that," Erik said.

"You will need to wash your hands very carefully. With soap," she said barely glancing up from the wound she was examining.

"My hands be clean."

"You can't always see the dirt. Do as I say. I don't have time for arguments."

Erik grunted in reply. Erin was glad he did as he was told.

She did the same despite having washed her hands at the women's camp. Rolling up her sleeves as far as it was decent she washed her arms as well. She'd forgotten Mick was standing near her. Looking up she caught him staring at the ugly scar on her arm. She quickly covered it.

"Nasty wound you got, Doc."

"It's nothing. Happened a long time ago." Erin quickly rinsed her hands checking her nails to ensure they were clean. "If you are going to assist me you need to wash up as well."

Mick took off his shirt rather than push his sleeves up. She took a deep breath trying to concentrate on making her patient feel comfortable. Karl had lost consciousness. Ellen wished Mick would put his shirt back on. The closeness of his naked torso was distracting at a time she needed her full attention.

"Please keep a close eye on his breathing. I am worried he may vomit from the combination of shock and whiskey. He could choke if he was still unconscious."

"Yes, Doc."

CHAPTER 29

Erik arrived back and insisted on showing her his washed hands. She smiled as he pointed out he had even washed his nails.

Taking scissors from her bag, she cut Karl's shirt away from the cut before asking Erik to undress him and wash his chest and all exposed skin. Erik looked at her dubiously but this time he didn't argue.

She poured hot water over the wound again and again. In between, she examined the wound to ensure she had removed any piece of bark, lint from the shirt and any other foreign object. Only when she was satisfied the wound was clean, could she start the process of setting the arm.

Erik moved the patient as she instructed while she poured water from every angle. Karl didn't make a sound until she had to use iodine. Then it was only a deep intake of breath. Her admiration for these men increased by the minute. She had seen qualified doctors scream when in less pain.

The bone was sitting at an awkward angle. Erin stared at it for a few minutes.

"Problem?" Mick asked her quietly.

She had forgotten he was there.

"I won't have the strength to set it properly," she admitted.

"Tell me how and I will do it."

She smiled at him gratefully. "You will need some help. Erik, can you find more men to help. Men like you who won't fall down when they see the blood."

Erik nodded. As he left to go find them, she called after him to tell the volunteers to wash up too.

Erin explained the process to Mick. She wasn't sure how much Karl understood but she thought she saw his eyes darken with fear. She couldn't blame him. Checking his forehead once more for signs of fever, he asked her something but she didn't understand. When Erik came back in she asked him to translate

"He wants to know when you take his arm off?"

"I'm not. Karl, by the time I am finished your arm will be perfect. It may be a little shorter than the other one but it will work just as well. So long as you do everything I say."

Erik translated, Karl looked at her with such

incredulity in his eyes she was stunned. If only she had known earlier what his fears were.

"I am going to use some ether to put you asleep. You have been very brave but this next bit will be too painful. It is better you sleep."

Karl nodded.

She took a small bottle out of her bag. After instructing Erik and Mick to stand back so they wouldn't be affected by the fumes, she carefully administered it to Karl. Once Karl was unconscious, she began instructing Mick and Erik how to help her. By the time Karl woke up, you could no longer see the bone. Erin was busy sewing up the wound. It was very hot in the tent and she had unbuttoned her shirtwaist as far as she dared. Mick came in with a cup of cool water which she gratefully accepted. She noticed he kept his eyes averted in deference to her modesty.

"Alicia is making you some food. She insists you need to rest."

"I need to put his arm in a splint first. Can you find me something suitable please?" she replied.

"Sure thing, boss," he grinned showing her, he was joking.

Karl smiled too. "Nice man you got. Pity, I would like to marry you."

Scarlet, Erin bent her head to concentrate on her sewing. She took a couple of deep breathes before realizing the smell of the oil in the canvas wasn't helping her stomach.

"These do?" Mick returned carrying some small shims and cardboard. She nodded not wanting to look up at him for fear he could see into her head.

"Karl, you need to keep this wound clean. It is very important. And you need to rest. No work for you not for at least two months. Then you can do something but not anything strenuous on your arm."

He didn't understand so she had Erik translate. She watched his reaction, knowing when Erik told him about not being able to work. Nobody in the camp could afford not to be earning.

"You come back with us to Clover Springs. I can look after you better and you can find a job," she said impulsively.

Karl smiled widely. She looked at Mick surprised to see him frowning. She would have thought he would have understood her reasons.

Anyway, she didn't have time to think about him now. She finished stitching up the wound, put on the splint and then went to wash her hands, neck, and arms as thoroughly as possible. She would have loved a bath.

"I'm sorry I couldn't go in and help you. I tried but there was too much blood," Alicia apologized.

"Don't worry, I have seen grown men faint at the

sight of blood. Thank goodness we were here. He would have lost his arm otherwise."

"He would have died you mean. Everyone is so happy you were here. You could set up your own practice and never run out of patients. "

Erin looked where Alicia was looking. A crowd of loggers had gathered. They all clapped for her. Embarrassed, she stood and bowed but they kept clapping.

Erik came forward and translated what they were cheering.

"They are very grateful. Karl has a child. His sister is raising the little girl as his wife died last year. He is a very popular member of the team."

"Has he agreed to come back to Clover Springs with us?" Erin asked.

Erik nodded. "I think the attraction might not be the town."

Erin blushed more at his teasing. Alicia laughed and then suddenly some music started. The men grabbed Alicia and Erin and the other woman and swung them around the camp. No longer exhausted, Erin joined in full of the joys of life. Until she spotted Mick standing outside the injured man's tent with his arms clasped tightly over his chest, his face like thunder. What was wrong with him?

CHAPTER 30

They waited a few days until Karl was well enough to travel and then made their way back to Clover Springs. Wilma introduced Karl to Mrs. Hofmeister. The poor woman was still struggling to tidy things up around the lumber mill. She obviously couldn't bear to think of selling it.

Erin hadn't planned on Karl being able to help the new widow but it looked like her idea was working well for both of them. Because of his size, Karl could carry a lot of things in his good hand. Erin came by to make sure he wasn't working too hard. He saluted her when he saw her. Mrs. Hofmeister was doing better too. Having a large man like Karl around meant Dickie and his friends didn't happen to drop by. Mick and the other men had filled the orders left behind when Hans died so she had money to make some of the repayments.

The clinic grew even busier. The women of Clover Springs seemed to have got over their reluctance at seeing a woman doc. They told her about their female problems and she commiserated with them. Despite knowing she didn't have children, the women seemed to think she understood everything involved in raising a family. Often the women weren't sick as such but just needed to offload their worries. Their husbands were usually too busy to listen to them and some of the things they told Erin, they couldn't tell their friends. If she had a dollar for every time she was told there were too many gossips in Clover Springs she would be a rich woman. But she wasn't. And while there were plenty of patients, she didn't know how she could afford to stay in Clover Springs. She couldn't live at the boarding house forever.

"Why don't you speak to my husband?" Emer suggested one day when Erin mentioned missing her own space. Erin looked at her blankly. "Shipley's bank. My husband Lawrence owns it."

"He's part of the Shipley banking family from Boston. Did you know them?" Alicia added.

Erin shook her head.

"He isn't going to lend me money. I am a woman."

"You are a doctor. My husband's different. If he wanted to be an old fashioned stick in the mud, he would have stayed in Boston with his mother." Emer's nose curled up slightly at the mention of her mother in law. "I will make an appointment for you for this afternoon. We aren't busy."

"But it's all so sudden."

"You can't hang around waiting for things to happen. You got to sort out your own luck," Emer answered as she finished mopping the floor with a flourish. "I'd hate to think what I'd be doing now if I had waited around."

"From what I've heard, you could be robbing the bank not be its owner," Alicia teased. Erin remained silent. She had so much to learn about all her new friends.

Going to the bank was risky. She couldn't lie to get a loan. She'd be committing fraud. But she couldn't tell the husband of the nurse she was working with the truth either. She decided to go and meet the banker. She could listen to what he said and make a decision later.

Once more she found herself wishing she'd been honest from the start. Living a lie made life very stressful.

* * *

The clinic was clean and tidy although a little on the small side. Emer went off to meet her husband and tell him he should back Erin. Erin tried to protest but Emer just laughed.

Alicia and herself sat down to enjoy a cup of tea and some cookies Alicia had brought with her. Alicia, in particular, was interested to discuss what improvements Erin thought they could make to the clinic.

"It would be nice to have some more private rooms and some indoor facilities. I don't like patients having to go outside when it is cold or wet," Erin suggested.

"We can do that," Alicia said excitedly. "We better speak to Doc as we don't want him thinking we are usurping his authority."

Erin was so grateful to the kindly old man. "He is such a nice old man, isn't he? He pretends to be grumpy but he has a heart of gold."

"It's like you have been here for years. You fit in so well."

Erin beamed at Alicia's comment. She did feel like this was home, something that scared her almost as much as it made her happy. She walked over to the stove to put some more logs on it. She didn't want Mrs. Grey catching a chill when she came in for her shift.

“Erin, I hope you don't think I am rude but are you and Mick Quinn, well do you have feelings about him?"

Erin hoped her red face would be put down to the heat. "Why do you ask?"

“You seem to enjoy his company."

"I do. He has been very nice, accompanying me on trips up to the loggers camp. I don’t know what I would have done without him. I don't think I could have got Michelle out of that place alive."

“Yes, he was very neighborly,” Alicia stared at her, a teasing glint in her eye. “But you haven’t answered my question."

“I don’t have time for romance. You can see how hard I work. I didn’t work so hard to become a doctor so I could stay at home polishing someone's boots."

“Well, it’s lovely to see my role as a mother and wife diminished to polishing boots."

"Oh Alicia, I am so sorry. I am far too direct. I didn't mean to insult you or any of the other wives and mothers here. I just meant it isn’t the role for me.”

Alicia smiled to show there were no hard feelings. Then she asked the question Erin dreaded. “So you don’t want children?”

Erin's heart twisted. "I would have loved to have children..." she said quietly. Alicia stared at her for a few moments, Erin was tempted to tell her but then common sense prevailed. "But I have another role now. I get to cuddle them and look after them but as soon as they turn cranky I hand them back to their parents."

"Hmmm, I don't think that is the full truth but I respect your privacy."

"So why ask me about Mick, I mean Mr. Quinn."

"I just wanted to... Oh, forget it."

"No, please, Alicia. You wanted to what?"

"Mick spends quite a bit of time at the Red Feather. Rumor has it he developed a love affair with one of the girls there, a girl called Mollie."

He had asked her to look after his woman. Of all the selfish, double-crossing... Erin kept her thoughts to herself. Adopting a face she used when she didn't want to alarm patients, she said, "So he wants to marry this girl? And you are afraid I will be hurt."

"I don't know if marriage is on the cards. Mick keeps his business fairly quiet. Aaron lived in the bunkhouse with him at the Sullivan ranch. Says he is a straight as a die but he thought he had family somewhere. I heard he was trying to buy Mollie's contract out."

Erin mulled that over for a couple of seconds before saying, "She is very young. Maybe he was trying to help her." Erin saw by the look on Alicia's face she didn't believe that. It did sound rather absurd.

"I hope you aren't cross with me saying something."

Erin smiled widely. "Of course not, Alicia, it means you are my friend. But please don't be worried, I haven't any intention of settling down with any man least of all Mick Quinn."

It just went to show you never could trust any man. No matter how nice and caring they seemed to be.

* * *

LATER THAT EVENING, she bumped into Mick.

"Evening Doc, how are you today?"

Think of the devil and he pops out behind you.

Erin forced a smile before turning to greet him.

"Fine thank you, Mr. Quinn. How are you?"

Satisfied she saw he was taken aback by her formal tone.

"You sure? You seem to be, well I don't know exactly," he looked as confused as he sounded.

"I'm a doctor, Mr. Quinn. I know when I am feeling fine. Goodnight."

"Night," he mumbled. She could feel him staring after her. A little piece of her felt bad for treating him so coldly but then thinking of him playing with her feelings and those of the poor young girl, she decided he deserved it. That girl was young enough to be his daughter for goodness sake.

CHAPTER 31

Mick was determined to find out why Doc Erin was treating him with cold indifference. They had been getting on so well. He thought they made some progress, especially during Karl's operation. She had been amazing, so calm and collected. He had got a bit of a shock walking into the tent and finding her in such a state of undress. He understood it was because of the heat but still it had unsettled him. She had such lovely skin. Apart from the burn he'd seen. She covered that up quickly though so he hadn't commented further on it. Was that why she was upset? Had he offended her in some way? He couldn't understand women. But he liked Erin. She was a good friend and he wanted to keep her as such.

"You busy today Doc?"

Erin looked up, she seemed surprised to see Mick standing in the door to the clinic but smiled when she saw the basket on his arm.

"Bit late for a picnic isn't it?" She said.

"Out here in Colorado you take advantage of every opportunity you can get. If you wrap up warm you won't feel the cold."

"Off you go, Doc Erin, you need some relaxation. If you get too cold, I am sure Mick can think of ways to warm you up."

"Wilma. If Mrs. Grey heard you saying things like that, she would have a fit."

"Mrs. Grey would give her full approval. She likes me," Mick added.

"Don't be too sure of that Mr. Quinn. What requires my approval?"

Erin turned bright red as Mrs. Grey walked into the clinic. "What's going on? Why is our good doctor in such a state?"

"Mick just invited the Doc for a picnic. I was just telling her she deserved to have a good time." Wilma's expression was so sweet, Mick had to look away.

"Hmm. Doc Erin does deserve a treat but you make sure you behave like a gentleman, Mick Quinn, or you will have me to deal with."

"Yes, ma'am," Mick said gravely as Erin got her cloak.

"Erin, I don't know what I did to upset you the other day but I just wanted to apologize," Mick said as he helped her into the wagon.

* * *

SHE IMMEDIATELY FELT GUILTY. She'd been the one who was cool with him following her conversation with Alicia. Maybe Alicia had gotten it wrong. From what she'd heard about Mick, he wasn't the type to take advantage of young girls. She decided to enjoy the day. Just because they were going for a picnic didn't mean he wanted to court her. Or me, him.

"I was rude. I shouldn't have snapped. Let's forget about it and enjoy the day," she said giving him a wide smile.

They didn't speak as he drove the wagon out to a pretty spot near the river.

"This is so beautiful and peaceful."

"I'm glad you like it. Wilma packed the picnic so you don't have to worry about being poisoned."

"Wilma was in on this picnic. But she looked so surprised when you came into the clinic," Erin said, not quite believing she had been so easily fooled.

"Course she was in on it. She had to be there to make sure the clinic wasn't left unattended. I didn't want to ask Mrs. Grey, she scares me."

Erin laughed at his admission. She didn't believe anyone scared Mick Quinn.

"Anyway, Wilma packs a better picnic than I do."

"I am sure you are capable of making a couple of sandwiches Mr. Quinn."

"Why can't you call me Mick. Mr. Quinn sounds so formal."

"Mick."

They chatted about this and that for a while before settling down to their picnic. Erin found herself telling him things about her family she had never really told anyone. Including the fact she and her Pa had been estranged when he died.

* * *

Mick was fascinated by every detail Erin revealed about herself. She missed her family, that much was obvious.

"Your da would be real proud of you," he said.

"How would you know?" she said using a smile to soften her next words. "Does being a man make you an expert on every man even those you have never met?"

"Nope, but your da was a fireman. He cared about people just like you do. He died trying to help people. If he could do that, he would be proud of his little girl helping others the way you do. Nothing seems to frighten you. You always do what is right for the patient regardless of the consequences."

"Thank you," she said softly tears making her eyes glisten. "I was on duty the night he died. By the time I got to see him, he was too far gone to be saved. I sat by his side willing him to regain consciousness so I could tell him I loved him. But he never did."

He cleared his throat. He hadn't wanted to stir up unhappy memories. Maybe he had been too personal in his observations but he liked seeing her smile. It brought her whole face alive.

"So did you always want to be a doctor? Didn't you ever want to get married and have a family." He knew immediately he'd said the wrong thing. She sat up straighter and started packing away their picnic.

"Yes, I always wanted to be a doctor. You know you should have your leg examined again? Would you like me to look at it for you?"

"Why?"

"They have learned a lot about leg injuries in the last twenty years. There may be ways of making it less painful."

"Who says its painful?" he almost growled. How did they get to the subject of his leg?

"You do, every time your face screws up when you put your full weight on it."

"You keeping a close eye on me, Doc?" His taunt hit the mark.

Her ears went pink as she pulled at the collar of her blouse. "No, it's my job to help people. You said so yourself."

"I said it was your job to help your patients. I ain't one of them." He stood up trying not to wince as the injury hurt. The pain made him cranky. "Don't you have enough patients to see without having to bully people into coming into the clinic."

"I am not bullying anyone. I merely suggested -"

"No thanks, but I appreciate the reminder I'm a cripple." He knew it wasn't fair but he was so angry he didn't really care.

"I never called you that name."

"Look Doc, I got lucky. Most men who were injured like I was, died. The surgeon who worked on me saved my leg and my life and for that I am grateful. But he didn't exactly do a neat job. It ain't pretty so nobody sees what it looks like."

"I am a doctor. I don't judge wounds on the basis of some beauty competition."

“So how do you judge people then? Because from where I am standing you set a fairly low bar."

* * *

SHE KNEW they were no longer talking about his leg but was rather mystified as to what exactly he meant.

"I don't follow you but you are obviously upset. I think its best if we headed back to town."

"I saw him walking you home," Mick snarled.

"Who?"

"Your new friend."

His snarky comments got her temper up. "You will have to be a little bit more specific. I am new to Clover Springs so that description could describe any one of a number of people."

"Dickinson. I saw him walking you home."

Horror dawned on her face. “He is not my friend. He walked me home one evening.”

“He held your arm. I saw it with my own eyes."

"And you accused me of paying close attention to your leg. Since when did it become any of your business, who escorts me anywhere. Of all the misguided...., " Erin couldn’t continue as she was afraid she would use unladylike language. "Please take me home."

"My pleasure." His face was like thunder but she was too wound up to care. How dare he accuse her of being friendly with the man who hurt Mollie and the other girls. Did he know nothing of her character?

The journey back to Clover Springs passed in silence and lasted what seemed like an eternity. She held herself rigid as he helped her down from the wagon. Without a word or a glance in his direction she walked into the Clinic and slammed the door shut behind her. Thankfully it was empty so there was nobody to see her behaving like a child.

CHAPTER 32

Minutes later, a banging on the door got her attention. If he thought he was going to apologize and they would be back being...

"Oh my God. What happened to her?"

Mick stood on the step, cradling an unconscious and badly beaten Mollie in his arms.

"Who did this to Mollie?"

"I found her collapsed outside on the street. Is she going to be all right?"

Erin couldn't give him false hope. The girl looked to be badly injured. "We won't know until I clean her up. If the injuries are superficial, skin deep, she will heal. But if there are internal injuries...." Erin didn't complete the sentence. Judging by the look on his face, she didn't have to.

"I'm going to kill him for this."

"No point in talking about that now. Carry her inside and lay her on the table please."

Mick watched as Erin carefully examined the young girl.

"Mick, can you get the bath down. We need to fill it with warm water. I have to wash the blood and grime away before I can tend to her properly." Erin spoke quietly her eyes full of unshed tears.

Mick nodded, he couldn't speak. He was glad there was something practical he could do. He wanted to go back to the Red Feathers and hang whoever was responsible from the balcony but that wouldn't help anyone.

"Will I go fetch Mrs. Grey or Mrs. Shipley?"

"No. Wilma. Get Wilma," Mollie murmured becoming agitated.

"Mick will get Wilma, Mollie darling. You got to stay as still as possible. I want to check for broken bones.

Mick walked as quickly as he could to the orphanage hoping to find Wilma alone. But Little Beaver was with her.

"Sorry to barge in but Doc Erin needs your help. Mollie got hurt. She's real bad." Mick failed to keep the panic from his voice.

Wilma stood. She grabbed her shawl from one peg before getting a bowl of something from the cupboard. "This will help her. It don't smell too good which is why I keep it covered. Nandita gave me some extra ingredients to improve on my ole Nanna's recipe."

Mick and Little Beaver followed after Wilma.

"You know who hurt her?" Little Beaver asked.

"Not yet, she ain't talking."

"But you think you know."

Mick stopped walking. "You and I know if it wasn't Dickie himself, it was one of his customers. He stood by while this happened. In my book that makes him as guilty as if he was the one who roughed her up."

Little Beaver looked stern. "Mick, leave this to the Sheriff."

"I don't know if I can do that."

Little Beaver's eyes showed he understood. "Do not go alone. If you have to do something make sure I am with you."

"Thank you, my friend."

Little Beaver followed Mick into the clinic but they didn't go into the examination room. They didn't have to, they could hear Mollie groaning from where they stood. Mick clenched and unclenched his fist. He couldn't bear to hear the girl in so much pain.

* * *

ERIN WASHED Mollie's body as gently as she could. She was covered in cuts and bruises, some showing the clear marks of fingerprints. Erin was most concerned about a nasty looking bruise around her stomach area. It was big enough to have been caused by a kick. She spoke to Mollie the whole time but the girl kept slipping in and out of consciousness. Wilma supported her head making sure her face was kept out of the water.

Only when she was washed and fully dried did they start rubbing in the salve. It stank to high heaven but Erin had known Wilma long enough to trust her.

"Last time we used this stuff was on Little Beaver's wife Asha. She was in a bad way and it made her better. Hopefully, it will do the same for Mollie." Wilma brushed Mollie's hair tenderly off her face. "You hear me, Mollie, you got to fight. Come back to us, please. Your friends are waiting to see you. You ain't never going back to that house, I swear to you, girl."

"How are we going to prevent him from taking her?"

"I don't know, Doc Erin, but slavery was abolished twenty years ago. She ain't going back there."

"Of course she ain't going back. I will kill Dickie first." Mick and Little Beaver came in once Mollie was decently dressed and in bed.

Erin moved toward Mick. "Please don't go near Dickie. At least not on your own."

"Don’t think I am man enough to face him?"

Erin took a step back from him, the anger in his tone matched by his face.

"My limp ain't never stopped me standing my ground. If you think I'm going to let him away with doing that, you don't know me at all."

"For goodness sake, your limp has nothing to do with it. Dickie is a dangerous man. He's going to be waiting for you. Mollie needs you here. You and Wilma are the only friends she's got. Put your stupid male pride aside for once and concentrate your energy where it's needed."

Erin stormed off on the pretext of getting something from another room but in reality, she had to get away. The girl's bruised and battered body was too familiar. She didn't have to imagine the pain she was in, she knew.

CHAPTER 33

"Mollie is very ill, Mick. I am..."

"She'll be fine, she's a fighter," Mick said not wanting to believe Erin's prognosis. He couldn't lose Mollie as well. "With all of you looking after her, how could she not get better?"

He didn't like the way Mrs. Grey, Emer, and Wilma wouldn't meet his eyes. He turned to Erin, her gaze was fixed on his but in a way, it was worse. Her eyes were full of compassion.

"Why don't you walk me back to the boarding house?" she suggested.

"Sorry Doc, I am staying here until she wakes up."

"She isn't going to wake up for a while. I sedated her to allow her body to heal." Erin picked up her cloak. "Come back with me and have some lunch. I hate to eat alone."

Mick didn't want to leave but at the same time, he didn't want to sit around staring at Mollie all day either. He had things to sort out.

"I will walk you back but I ain't in the mood for lunch. I got stuff to do anyway," he said.

"Mick, please don't go to see Dickinson. Leave him for the law to sort out."

Mick couldn't miss the pleading in her eyes. She did care for him. Whether as a friend or more, he wasn't sure but it wasn't time to be thinking of that now.

"I ain't going near Dickie. I need to go speak to Cookie."

He walked Erin back to the boarding house, thankful she was quiet too.

"Are you sure you won't have something to eat?" she asked.

"I couldn't stomach anything but thanks."

Erin smiled a sad smile before going in and closing the door behind her.

* * *

Mick walked slowly to the telegraph office. He knew Cookie would agree with what he was doing. He had been tellin' him for long enough to cut his ties with

Virginia. He should have done it earlier. Then he would have been able to buy Mollie out of her contract and she wouldn't be lying in the clinic at death's door. He had let her down just as much as his sisters.

He sent the telegram to the Stephenson family to say the farm was up for sale. He knew they would jump at the chance to buy it. He trusted them to arrange everything at their end. He called into the bank to see what he needed to do. Then he took his horse and headed out to see Cookie. He needed the older man's calming influence.

* * *

ERIN DIDN'T EAT MUCH and sleep eluded her. She washed and returned to the clinic. There was no change in Mollie. Why hadn't she done something? She knew the girl was in danger yet she hadn't rescued her.

"This ain't your fault, Doc Erin," Wilma said softly as they sat either side of Mollie's bed. "The only one responsible is Dickie."

"I should have made more of an effort to keep her safe."

"You did all you could and more. The girls told me how you stood up to Dickinson. How you got them regular meals, hot water and all. Not many people would do anything like that for soiled doves."

"But it wasn't enough, was it?" Angrily Erin dashed the tears from her eyes. It wouldn't do any good crying about it. This was real life out West. No different from back East really. Some lives just weren't important enough to matter. Whether they be penniless immigrants off the boat, war veterans whose injuries prevented them from working so their families went hungry or young girls like Mollie lured into prostitution on the pretext of a better life. There had to be something she could do.

She stood up. Her mam said there was always something to be done. She just had to find it.

"Where you going Doc? You got a look on your face that means trouble."

"I am not sitting here while he goes scot free. I am going to find Mr. Dickinson and have him arrested for the murder of Kathryn and the attempted murder of Mollie."

"But no body was ever found."

"He doesn't know that. He said she got the train out of Clover Springs. We both know Matthews is way too noisy to miss a soiled dove attempting to ride his train without a ticket. "

"I is coming with you." Wilma stood up.

"Wilma, sit down and mind Mollie."

* * *

DETERMINED TO FIND DICKINSON, Erin knew she first had to locate Little Beaver and the sheriff. The Indian had warned her they had to play by the book if they ever wanted to get Dickinson. Well, she didn't have to tell them everything, did she? First, she went home and found what she was looking for. Then she went to the jailhouse where she found both of them.

"Sheriff, Little Beaver, I need you to arrest Dickinson for murder."

"Murder Doc. That's a big leap." The sheriff stood all the same.

"Did Mollie die?" Little Beaver asked.

"No, although she is gravely ill. I am going to confront Dickinson now. I want you to come with me and hear his confession."

With that, she turned on her heel and made her way down the street toward the saloon. She knew without looking back, the two lawmen would follow her. As before she stopped just at the entrance but this time she needed to calm her temper. Taking a few deep breathes, she walked into the saloon.

"Everyone out. I want to speak to Dickinson alone," she ordered.

"You gone plum crazy, Doc. You can't throw everyone out." The barkeep barely looked at her.

"Ok, maybe I will have to persuade you." Erin took the gun out of her pocket and fired a shot into the air. The crowd scattered.

"Dickinson, I know you are back there. Come out here where I can see you."

"Doc Erin, you can't go around shooting at ceilings," Little Beaver protested.

"That's okay. I'm not aiming at the ceiling next time." Erin replied, aiming her gun at Dickinson's chest.

He grinned at her. "Now little lady, why don't you put that thing away. Everyone knows you don't know how to use it."

"That's true, Mr. Dickinson. I am not a crack shot. But I guess even this little lady could do a lot of damage just pointing it and pulling the trigger. Do you want me to check?"

Dickinson blanched, obviously realizing she was serious.

"Doc, calm down now. You can't go around threatening people. That's against the law."

"The law!" she screamed at him. "How dare you quote the law at me. I have Mollie in my clinic and she'll be lucky if she lives to see nightfall."

"Mollie's dying?" Lily came out from the shadows.

"Get out of here, Lily, ain't no business of yours. Dusty, take her out back."

"You lay a hand on me, Dusty, and I swear I will tear your eyes out." Lily looked so threatening, Dusty took a step back.

"What do you want Doc? It ain't my fault a customer got a little carried away."

"There isn't a place on that girl that isn't covered in a wound or bruises. Do you know how old she is? Fourteen. Yeah, you heard me. Same age as your daughter, Mr. Larkin. A year older than yours, Clay. " She didn't look at the father's whose names she called out. Her attention was focused solely on Dickinson.

"You are responsible. You let this happen. You murdered Kathryn and now Mollie could die. I reckon you should be strung up from the nearest tree."

The men behind her murmured. It was obvious to everyone the crowd was growing in number and they weren't happy.

"I told you, Doc. Kathryn took a train out of here and went back to her hometown."

"You're lying. Her body was delivered to my clinic just the other night. I've been carrying out a post mortem trying to establish the cause of death. It's difficult to work out which blow killed her."

Erin let the implication sink in. The crowd's mutterings grew louder. She saw Dickinson exchange a look with Dusty who shrugged his shoulders. He was the weak link.

"Little Beaver keep an eye on Dickinson, please. Make sure he doesn't move."

Little Beaver moved up beside Dickinson. He stood with his arms crossed, a furious expression on his face. Erin turned her attention to Dusty. She aimed a shot at the floor near his boot. He yelped.

"Mind where you're shooting that thing." he cursed at her.

"I was aiming for the floor. Next time I will aim a little higher." She waved the gun in the general direction of his middle. "Even a child who has never fired a gun before can kill a man by aiming for his stomach. A stomach wound is never treatable. Death generally comes very slowly as you lie in agony. Your guts...."

"Stop, Doc, you made your point. What do you want?"

"Who killed Kathryn?" Erin pretended to adjust her aim. "Did she backchat you just that one time too many?"

"Shut up, Dusty," Dickinson called.

Erin pretended not to hear. Still playing with the gun, she spoke conversationally. "The girls told me about your problem. How it takes you so long to ...." Erin looked at him pointedly.

Dusty broke. “It was him. He did it. Some fella complained she'd stolen his watch. Dickie got really mad, worse than I ever seen him before. He took her down the basement."

"Shut up, Dusty. I'm warning ye. I'll string you up myself."

Dusty went white looking at Dickie. Erin fired another shot in the direction of his feet. This one hit him in the boot.

"You trying to kill me?"

"I'm just getting your attention. He might be threatening to kill you but I actually got the means to do it right here in my hand. My finger is a bit twitchy too. The gun keeps going off." Erin twirled the gun again praying it wouldn't go off. She hadn't meant to hit him last time.

"Sheriff, stop her."

"I can't disarm her and I refuse to shoot a lady. You best tell her what she needs to know mister."

"He did it. I buried the body right over at the old Oak tree You know the one, on the way out of the town toward the river. I was going to move it later but ..."

"You can't believe a word he's saying. He is just trying to save his neck. You ain't got witnesses."

"Yes, they do. I saw him dragging the body."

"Shut up, Lily, nobody going to believe a two-bit ..."

Lily moved fast. She hit Dickinson a slap right across the face. "I know what I am but at least I can sleep peacefully at night. Where you're going, you ain't ever going to rest easy."

"Little Beaver arrest those two men. Ma'am we are going to have to take your statement. Are there any other witnesses?"

"A whole houseful, Sheriff." Lily winked at Doc Erin. Erin had to look away. She couldn't condone perjury but she wasn't going to lose sleep over the girls lying to get Dickinson convicted. He was guilty and they all knew it.

"Doc Erin, I have to arrest you too."

"Sheriff, you can't arrest the doc. She's got patients to see to. Without her, Mollie will die," Lily pleaded.

"In that case, I am placing you under house arrest at the clinic. I will tell Mrs. Grey to keep a close eye on you. But I will need your gun."

"With pleasure. I hate those things."

CHAPTER 34

Against all the odds Mollie survived. She gained more strength with every day that passed. Her broken arm would never be fully straight again but apart from that and a few discolored bruises, she looked almost as good as she had before her injuries.

"Doc Erin, I don't know how I can thank you for what you've done. I wish I could be like you."

"You can, Mollie. There is nothing to stop you. I've seen you reading. You are a very intelligent girl."

"No way I could go to school, not now." Mollie's eyes darkened.

Erin put a finger under her chin. "Look at me. You are not to look to the past but to the future. You would make an amazing doctor as you know what it is really like to suffer. You have a big heart too."

"But how? I can't afford to go to school."

"Yes, you can. We are going to help you. Wilma has a friend who lives out in Santa Fe. It's far enough away for nobody to know you. You can be free, Mollie. You will never forget what happened to you but you can use your experiences to help others."

"I could be a doctor?"

"Or a teacher or a nurse. Wilma's friend used to work in a house like the Red Feathers. She now runs a home for girls who got in trouble. Not all of them worked as you did. Some of them had babies and their families threw them out. Others are orphans. Whatever the reason, she never turns anyone away. Wilma sent her a telegram and she replied to say she can't wait to meet you."

"How will I get to Santa Fe? It's miles away."

"Mick..." Erin paused as Mollie's face lit up and she interrupted.

"Mick is taking me?"

"No, Mollie. Mick has his own stuff to attend to. Mick's friend Cookie offered to escort you there."

"Oh." Mollie looked so crestfallen, Erin wanted to cheer her up but she didn't know how.

"Where is Mick going?"

"He said something about Virginia." Erin wasn't sure what Mick was doing but he had to go away for a couple of weeks. "I think he might have decided to find his family. You know he has a wife and kids."

"Yeah, he told me." Something about Mollie's facial expression made Erin wonder but then Wilma distracted both of them.

"Mollie, you got a visitor."

Wilma stood back to let a young woman come in. At first glance, Erin didn't recognize Lily.

"Lily, you look amazing. You are really pretty in that dress."

"Thanks, Mollie. Mrs. Grey got it for me. She got me a whole lot of stuff."

Erin hugged Lily close. "Thank you for everything you did."

Lily shrugged but Erin could see she was pleased.

"Thank you, Lily. Doc Erin told me how you stood up and told the Judge all about what Dickie did to me and the other girls. And to Kathryn." Mollie's voice caught on a sob.

"Poor Kathryn. She should have left when she got the chance," Lily said "But she stayed to help us. She was determined we would all escape one day."

"Well, she succeeded, didn't she? Are you sure you want to go to New York, Lily? You could go to Santa Fe with Mollie."

"I'm sure. I got a brother in New York. He has a wife and a family. I wrote to him and he said I was welcome to come to live with them. He don't know anything about what happened to me."

Erin got the impression Lily was lying but she wasn't sure why. Erin hugged Lily closer. "You weren't responsible for what happened. Dickinson was. If you don't live your life to the max, he'll have won."

"How come you know so much about what we went through, Doc Erin?" Lily asked making Mollie stare at her.

"I didn't work in a house like you girls did but someone treated me just like Dickie treated you. You cannot let men like him win. No matter who they are."

The girls nodded solemnly, nobody saying anything. They were all caught up in their own world.

* * *

MICK RACED to the train station desperate not to miss Mollie's departure. He'd thought Erin was joking when she said the younger girl was leaving today. He'd only come back from Virginia yesterday. He'd wanted to call in on Erin to tell her how he felt about her. How he'd sold the farm and would use the proceeds to buy them a house in Clover Springs. She could continue being the town doctor and he would find something.

He'd planned to ask her to marry him. Mollie could

live with them until she decided what her future held. He'd been so shocked by the fact Mollie was leaving, he hadn't got a chance to speak to Erin properly. She'd been rather standoffish. It wasn't exactly the warm welcome he'd been hoping for. But he would sort it out once he said goodbye to Mollie. Maybe Erin was jealous of the younger girl. Some people thought he wanted to marry Mollie.

"Matthews, I just have to say goodbye to someone," he shouted as he climbed on board. Walking through the cars, he finally spotted Mollie and Cookie sitting ahead of him.

Both stood up as he approached them.

"You weren't going to leave without saying goodbye were you, Moll?"

Mollie turned away so he couldn't see her face. When he gently turned her back, he saw she had been crying. He gently wiped them off her cheeks.

"Why?" he asked.

"You know why. After what I said?"

"You told me you loved me. I love you darling but as a little sister. I never want to lose contact with you."

"Then let me stay with you."

Mick knew he had to be the strong one for both of them. "Mollie, you got a chance to go to school. To make something of your life. You deserve so much better than a life here in Clover Springs. Here some will never let you forget about the past."

"But I would be with you."

He tilted her chin so she looked up into his face. "You need a man who loves you like a man not like a brother. You deserve a happy family. Your future is so bright Mollie, can't you see?"

"I'm scared."

"I know you are, sweetheart, but Cookie, he's the nearest thing I have to a father. He's going to look after you. He won't let anything bad happen on the trip I promise."

"But Dickie..."

"He won't ever get out of prison. If he did, he still won't find you. You have a new name and a new place to live. Wilma knows the lady you are going to stay with. She wouldn't let you go anywhere if it was dangerous."

Mollie looked unconvinced.

"Come on Moll, where's that fighting spirit gone. You got to go show people what you are made of."

"Will you write to me?"

"Yes, of course, I will. Lots."

She smiled at last, "Don't lie, but once or twice a year would be nice."

Mick smiled "You know me so well. I will write at least twice a year I promise."

"You going to ask the lady doc to marry you?"

Mick's smile faltered. How did Mollie know anything about that?

"Don't look so surprised. I seen the way you look at her. I spent ages wishing you would look at me that way."

"She ain't interested in me."

"That's 'cause she thinks you got a wife and family already but you ran out on them."

Mick stared at her, not believing what he just heard. "She thinks what? Why?"

Mollie looked everywhere but at him.

"What did you do Moll?"

"I didn't tell her the story, she heard it somewhere. But I didn't tell it was a lie either. I'm sorry Mick. I thought if she wasn't interested then you would let me stay. Don't be angry please."

Mick saw the desperation and loneliness in her face and his temper died as fast as it had risen. "Come here you." He pulled her into his arms and gave her a long steady hug.

"One day you will see what you feel for me is what is natural for a big brother. A man, a good one, will come along and sweep you off your feet. You will fall in love, get married and have a family. But only after you get a decent education first mind."

"Yes, Pa. " She joked. He was relieved

He wasn't sure if she would ever recover enough to let herself have the happiness a family unit could bring but that was up to her. He had done all he could. Now he had to sort out the mess he'd made of his own life.

The train whistle announced its departure. He gave Mollie another hug before turning to shake Cookie's hand. The older man followed him to the door as he jumped out of the car.

"I'll look after her. Now go get that lady but don't you dare have the wedding till I am back you hear?"

The train pulled out of the station. He watched it leave taking the time to arrange his thoughts. He had to find a way of convincing Erin he loved her. But how…

CHAPTER 35

Mick knocked on the door of the clinic hoping to find Erin alone. She was and it was obvious she'd been crying.

"You missing her already?" he said gently.

"Yes. I know she needs a fresh start and Wilma's friend will look after her but she looked so young leaving here. I hope she will be okay."

"She will be fine, she knows she can come back if she wants to. We will always have a home waiting for her."

Erin smiled but the smile slid off her face as she seemed to register what he had said.

"Pardon," she whispered.

He thought he saw panic in her eyes. It couldn't be. Surely she knew he had been leading up to this moment.

"Erin, sit down. I have something to tell you. You may have heard the rumors about my having a family."

Erin didn't sit, she moved from one thing to another. He was getting dizzy watching her move so quickly. He reached out and pushed her gently onto a seat. He took the one opposite her. "Have you heard gossip about my family?”

Erin looked at a spot above his face. "Mollie may have mentioned something."

"I had a family. Before the war." He took the photograph out and handed it to her. She stared at it before looking at him in shock. "This looks just like Mollie."

"Her name is... was Susanna."

"She died in the war?" Erin asked softly still examining the picture.

"I don't know. All I know is Pa died on the battlefield, Ma died from some sort of fever at our farm and nobody knows what happened to the girls. I like to think they were adopted by someone kind but I don't think I will ever know."

She looked at him, unshed tears making her eyes shimmer. "I am very sorry Mick. Have you been looking for them all this time?"

"Yes, but I have to stop living in the past. The Stevenson's bought my farm."

At her perplexed expression, he explained how the Stephensons had been renting the farm. They had wanted to buy it for a long time but he didn't feel it was right to sell. His sisters may come back.

"But I realized, well Cookie told me if my sisters ever returned the Stephenson's would tell me."

"Did you not want to settle on the farm yourself. Raise your own family?" She asked, looking at the photo again.

"Erin, I don't think I could have a family. The injury I have may have prevented that. It is important I marry a woman who isn't looking to have children of her own. One that has a career she is already married too."

Erin dropped the photo. They both bent to pick it up, bringing their faces close together. He leaned in and stole a kiss. She surprised him by kissing him thoroughly as if she would never get enough of him. It left him shaken to the core but with a feeling of foreboding rather than desire.

"Erin, I think you know what I am trying to say..."

She stood up again, wiping her hands down her dress over and over.

"Erin... will you?"

"Don't ask me, please. Why did you have to bring this up now? Why couldn't you leave things as they were? We were friends, good friends. Isn't that enough?"

He stood. "Not for me. I love you, Erin Brennan. I

want to spend the rest of my life loving you. I sold the farm and bought the Red Feathers"

Stunned she whirled around. "You did what?"

"I thought it would make a good house for anyone who needs our help. Young girls like Mollie who don't have anywhere to turn. I thought Lily might stay and help us run it. We could even look at adopting Michelle."

'Lily is going to New York to her brother."

"Is that what she told Mollie? That's not true. Her brother sent her a telegram telling her, his sister was dead. Seems he blames her for the life she led even if it wasn't her fault."

"Oh no, poor Lily. I must find her and make sure she knows she can stay here. "

"Find her in a bit. I know Lily is important but so are we. So, Doc Erin, are you going to marry me?"

He saw the blood drain out of her face as she stared at him. "I can't marry you. I'm sorry Mick. I am never getting married."

A knocking on the clinic door interrupted them.

"Doc Brennan, they called an urgent town meeting. You're needed," a man she didn't recognize said.

"Is someone hurt, did something happen?"

"Don't know. I was just sent to find you and make sure you came back with me."

"Let me get my bag. " Erin picked up her bag. She turned to face Mick. "I'm sorry."

And then she was gone.

It took Mick more than a few seconds to follow after her. He didn't catch up until they got to the church where a large crowd had gathered. What on earth was going on?

CHAPTER 36

Mick pushed his way inside, seeing Erin at the top of the church beside Charlie Staunton.

"Doc Brennan, nice of you to join us." Charlie Staunton smiled making Mick nervous. The man never smiled. What was he up to?

"You may remember I wasn't in agreement with the town having a lady doctor?"

"We all know that Staunton. But you have been proved wrong. Doc Erin has been an asset to this town in more ways than one. She is an excellent doctor." The old doc took his seat once more.

Mick saw Erin send the old doctor a quick look of gratitude. Then her concentration returned to Staunton.

"Yes, well, that is a matter of opinion. Let's stick to

the facts, shall we? Where did you say you went to medical school Doc Brennan?"

"New York," Erin spoke quietly.

"Then explain why the medical college at Syracuse has never heard of a student called Erin Brennan."

Erin went white, he saw her hands grip her skirt. She looked completely terrified. He stared at Staunton, in contrast, the man looked almost jubilant as he waved the piece of paper in front of him.

"Well, Doc Brennan, we are waiting."

"I did attend the medical school and was a month away from passing my final exams."

"So you are not a real doctor after all."

"I was going to pass, all my lecturers told me. Based on my previous..."

"But you didn't sit the exam, did you? Can I ask why?"

Mick wanted to bundle Erin out of the room. It was obvious Charlie knew the answer to his question.

"The governors of the College wouldn't allow me too."

"Because you were a divorced woman or because you were a killer?" Staunton spat out. "No wonder you were so keen to take on Dickinson by yourself. He wasn't the first person you threatened to kill was he?"

Divorced? A killer? Mick stared at Erin, the truth was written all over her face. Murmurs went up around the hall as people whispered, some discretely, but most were quite loud.

"I think we better let Miss Brennan explain herself." Father Molloy's voice rang out over the crowd. Mick didn't miss the fact he referred to Erin as Miss rather than the usual doctor. He guessed from the reaction of the crowd he wasn't the only one.

Erin closed her eyes for a couple of seconds, her mouth moving as if she was praying. She then squared her shoulders and walked toward Father Molloy. On reaching his side, Mick was relieved to see the Priest clasp her hand. He was standing by her. No matter what. Mick wished he could stand up with them but that would only cause more talk. Wouldn't do Miss, Doc Brennan's reputation any good either.

"I didn't kill anyone. That court case was a result of the actions of grieving parents who happen to have a lot of influence in New York." The murmurs around the hall got louder. He watched Erin carefully. Everything about her screamed she was telling the truth but it was a difficult tale to tell.

"I divorced my husband in my final year of medical school." The room went silent as people digested the statement. A husband. She'd been married before. Why didn't she say anything?

"The case attracted a lot of press attention mainly because of who my husband was. His family is well known. The day the divorce was granted my husband died. I was accused of his manslaughter. I was found innocent."

"So you got away with it. And decided you'd come here pretending to be a doctor. You're a charlatan," Staunton mocked. Mick was tempted to wring his neck.

"As I said, I was less than a month away from my final exams when I was asked to leave. In the eyes of the law I was innocent but some, quite a few, to be honest, believed I had done it."

"I don't believe you're innocent. You showed up here claiming to be a doctor. You tricked all of us. That ain't the actions of someone with nothing to hide."

Mick waited to hear what Erin said even though he agreed with Staunton. As he looked around the room, he saw a lot of other people nodding their heads. Wilma and Mrs. Grey were both looking at Erin as if they were statues, there wasn't a shred of emotion on either of their faces.

"I realize how my actions look. However, if I had told you the truth would you have given me a chance? I fully intended going back to school and completing my exams but I..."

"Decided to live as a fraud instead. Here in Clover Springs." Staunton's gloating tone made Mick want to punch him.

“I swear to you, Father Molloy, and the rest of you, I didn't mean to act in such a disgraceful manner. I had no other option. I worked hard to become a doctor. I believe I am a good one. My husband wasn’t a pleasant man. He was difficult, controlling and had many enemies. It might have been easier if I had murdered him. But, I couldn’t kill him much as I may have wanted him dead."

Shocked intakes of breath greeted her remarks.

"I am sorry but you asked for the truth. I made the biggest mistake of my life marrying a brute. I wasn’t prepared to let him win. I am a doctor.”

"An excellent one too. Before you people get all uppity, put yourself in Doc Erin’s shoes. Would you have let her near you Mr. Larkin if you knew her history?” Mr. Larkin shook his head at Mrs. Grey’s question.

“No. Then you would be dead,” Mrs. Grey continued. “Or you, Mrs. Flanagan? When I couldn’t birth your baby, Erin saved both you and your son. Would you have let her into your house if you had known she hadn’t finished school?”

Mrs. Flanagan looked everywhere but at Mrs. Grey.

“I don’t agree with lying. I am as shocked as the rest of you." Mrs. Grey glanced at Erin.

Mick saw Erin wince, her eyes clouded with pain.

"However, after working very closely with Doc Erin over the last few months and seeing the number of patients her knowledge has helped, I believe we should let her stay in Clover Springs."

"But she lied.." Staunton protested.

" You have never given her a chance, not from the first day she walked into this town." Mick stood up.

"Just because I don't behave like a lovesick puppy dog following her around all the time. Aren't you content with your soiled dove or is it a haram you're after?"

Mick's punch connected with Staunton's cheek.

"Stop it. At once." Erin's voice stopped both men in their tracks. "I was wrong. I should have told the truth from the start. I should have trusted you. I am sorry. Believe me, you don't know how sorry. Erin turned to Mrs. Sullivan. "I will be packed and out of the boarding house within the next twenty-four hours. I'm sorry," she whispered one more time before fleeing the building.

Mrs. Grey and Mrs. Sullivan went to follow her but Father Molloy stopped her. "Leave her alone for a little while. I think she needs it." Father Molloy's voice was as sad as the look on his face.

"We can't sit around here just leaving her over there by herself. We all got a past. Not nobody here who never made a mistake before. Not even you, Father."

"Wilma. You can't say things like that to a priest."

"Why not Mrs. Shaw? I'm as fallible as the next man. Thank you, Wilma, for your reminder. We all need to look at our own actions before we judge those of others."

"So can she stay? I like having a female doc around. She's easy to talk to and she doesn't mind if it takes a while for me to get to the point." A glare in Doc's direction followed Mrs. Flanagan's remark. "She saved my baby. Mrs. Grey was right about that. She's a good doctor. I don't need a piece of paper to see that. Couldn't read it anyway." Mrs. Flanagan laughed but whether she was amused or nervous Mick couldn't tell.

"I appreciate you sharing your opinion Mrs. Flanagan. Now is not the time to be making decisions. We have to see whether Miss Brennan wants to stay or not."

"Doc Brennan and she ain't going nowhere. I refuse to let anyone in this town bully her out." Wilma glared at Charlie Staunton, Mrs. Shaw and the other people flanking him. "If you make the female doc leave, I is going too."

"Now Wilma, steady on. We don't have to do anything hasty," Father Molloy said.

"I'm with Wilma," Mrs. Grey stepped forward. "And so will every decent person in this town. So the girl didn't tell us the whole truth. But how many of us assumed she was here as a new bride when she first arrived. We didn't exactly insist she show us paper qualifications. As Doc says, she's an excellent doctor. That's high praise coming from him." Mrs. Grey's tone brooked no argument.

Doc nodded but didn't add anything more to the conversation. Mick had heard enough.

CHAPTER 37

He marched down the station. He knew the minute she saw him as she took a step back, the fear on her face making him pause.

"We need to talk. You and I got unfinished business." He took her arm, gently but firmly steering her off the platform toward a quiet part of the street. "Matthews mind the Doc's bags," Mick shouted to the station master staring after them.

Erin didn't say a word, her white face making her blue eyes look almost violet.

"Why are you running away? Stay here and fight. You said Clover Springs felt like home."

Erin didn't answer.

"What are you so afraid of? I've seen you take on almost everyone other people would walk two blocks to avoid. So I know you aren't a coward. Do you not feel the same as I do?"

He moved closer to her, the look in his eyes daring her to lie.

"No. I ..."

"No? Really. You don't feel like you will stop breathing if you never saw me again?"

She dragged her gaze away from his.

"I don't feel like that."

"I don't believe you. You're lying but I don't know why? Is it because you think you are too good for a cowboy?"

Stunned, she looked back into his eyes. "Of course not, that's got nothing to do with it."

He stared at her for a couple of seconds, she wouldn't return his gaze.

"Why didn't you tell me? You let me make a fool of myself all this time."

"Nobody knew."

* * *

THE STRICKEN look in his eyes made her feel even worse. "Do you think I care whether people knew or not. I loved you and you let me believe I had a chance."

"No, I didn't"

"Don't lie, not again."

She caressed the tops of her arms trying to put into words what she'd sworn she'd never talk about again.

"So, you are a widow. You could have told everyone. Being a widow is respectable"

She didn't answer.

"I asked you a question. Why didn't you trust me enough to tell me?" He moved closer as he raised his voice

Instinctively she shrank back.

"That mark on your shoulder, It wasn't an accident, was it? " "No," she shouted back at him.

"Erin, come and sit down, You're shaking. Here take my jacket." He wrapped his jacket gently around her shoulders. "I'm sorry I raised my voice. I had no right."

"I should have been honest but for a while, I just wanted to be me. Not the girl who was always on the wrong side. My da didn't want me to be a doctor, he wanted me to settle down and get married, have a family. That was what good Irish Catholic girls did."

"So you married to please your da?"

"In a way, I wish I could say yes but that isn't the truth. I thought I was in love. I married a doctor. I thought he believed in everything I did. He said he had no problem with female doctors. He didn't unless they were his wife."

"A doctor did that to your skin?" Mick fought hard to control his feelings.

Erin nodded. "Anthony had a patient, a child. He became very ill. Anthony was supposed to be on duty but ... Anyway, I had to do something. I performed a tracheotomy."

"I don't know what that is. Did the patient die?"

"I cut a hole in his windpipe to allow him to breathe. No, he survived."

"So why was your husband angry? "

"Because it looked bad. The doctor in charge of the hospital wanted to know why Antony had left me alone. I wasn't supposed to be on the wards on my own never mind doing surgery."

"Where was he?"

"It doesn't matter. When we got back to our house, Anthony decided it was all my fault. I had deliberately set out to ruin his career. He became very angry. That was the first time he hit me."

"Did you report him to the police?

"I spoke to a policeman who had been friends with my da. He told me all men had to get used to being married. Things would settle in time especially when I gave him a son. I never fell pregnant. Yet another way I failed as a wife." A tear trickled down her cheek.

"Erin, it might not have been you who couldn't have children."

“Anthony insisted it was. The lack of children made him worse. I think. The day after he burnt my upper arm, I filed for divorce.”

"Did you not tell your Ma or the rest of your family?"

"No, by the time Anthony started hitting me, Da had died. Mam was mourning her husband, she had enough to deal with. She decided it would be easier to go back to Ireland. I couldn’t tell her I was leaving my husband, she would have been so upset. Irish people don't get divorced, not our type anyway. So Mam made her preparations to go back to Ireland. I knew as soon as she went I would leave. But Anthony found out. I still don't know how I suspect it was one of his servants. He met me at the ship knowing, I suppose, I would put on the loving wife act for Mam. She was so happy I was well looked after.”

"So she left and you went home with him."

"I didn’t realize how angry he was. As soon as the front door closed I realized I had made a huge mistake. He'd given the staff the night off. It was only the two of us in the house.”

"Oh Erin, why didn’t you just tell me. I would have understood.”

"No, you wouldn’t. Nobody knows what it is like to have the person you love turn into a monster right in front of your eyes. Anthony was a well-respected doctor. The staff at the hospital loved him, the nurses in particular. He was charming and came from a highly thought of medical family. His father was a doctor as was his father. Even after he died, his family sent men after me."

"Surely they must have seen the bad side of him?"

"No, he kept that well-hidden. It only came out later at the trial."

"Antony was very angry when the Judge said he would grant the divorce. He became very vocal in court and accused me of all sorts of things including trying to poison him. He said if anything ever happened to him, they would know who to blame."

"And?"

"And Anthony went out that night and shot himself. After everything, I went through the scandal of becoming a divorced woman. He killed himself anyway. The divorce hadn't been finalized. His death meant I was free, I was a respectable widow." Her fury at the injustice she had suffered made her voice shake. Tears flowed down her face. "But I wasn't free. His family are powerful people. I was arrested on a charge of manslaughter."

"But surely it was obvious he killed himself?"

Erin stared at him.

"In the eyes of many people I was responsible for my husband's death. I had goaded him by insisting on working as a doctor rather than staying home to mind the house. I was lucky though. I had an understanding Judge who saw the case for what it was. He said I was innocent of all charges. " Erin took a deep breath.

"But it didn't matter. My life was ruined. Anthony got his revenge. The hospital where I worked refused to let me complete my training. All those years of hard work meant nothing. Nobody else would give me a job."

"So you came here?"

"I had a package for Father Molloy from my mam. I intended delivering it and then making my way onto Denver. I was going to try to find work as a doctor or nurse. Anything to pay the bills."

"Father Molloy must have recognized you?"

"He did but he never knew I was married. Brennan is my maiden name."

"Come here, Erin." He pulled her to him and cuddled her as she cried and cried. He kept holding her in silence letting her release all her pent up emotions.

"I'm sorry for lying to you as well. When we met and I … began to have feelings for you, I got scared. I was going to tell you but then one thing after another happened. It was never the right time."

"I wish you had trusted me but your story doesn't

change my feelings. I still want to marry you, Erin. I love you."

"I love you too but I can't get married. Never again. I loved Anthony with all my heart or at least I thought I did. Look at how well that turned out."

He wasn't impressed at being compared to someone who sounded like a walking maniac but he, sort of, understood her reasoning.

"Erin Brennan or whatever your name is. I don't take no for an answer. I spent years looking for my family. I am not going to let this chance of happiness go. However long it takes, I am going to get you to become Mrs. Quinn. But for now, I'll settle for a kiss and something to eat. I'm starving."

Erin hiccuped then laughed. He kissed her gently on the lips.

"Mick, anyone could see us."

"Darling after that town meeting, I doubt anyone has time to talk about a kiss. They'll be much more interested in the killer Doc on the loose in Clover Springs."

"Oh, you." She pushed him but gently. He noticed she didn't let his hand go but held onto it firmly. He would get her to become his wife no matter how long it took. She was a woman worth waiting for.

EPILOGUE

Mick walked back and forth.

"You goin' to wear the carpet out. Quit pacing," Cookie instructed.

"I ain't pacing."

"Yup. You are."

"What's taking so long? She said she'd be here at one. Do you think she's run out on me?"

Cookie laughed causing Mick to glare at him. "Some friend you are. I'm in distress and you think it's amusing."

"You and Doc Erin are never apart. All of Clover Springs know it. Your soon to be wife just had a clothing crisis. It happens to all brides."

"You sound very knowledgeable for an old bachelor."

"Hey less of the old and as for the bachelor bit, I'm working on that."

Mick saw Cookie winking at Mrs. Higgins who blushed like a young girl. He hoped it would work out for his friend and Mrs. H. He loved both of them and wanted them to be happy.

Father Molloy coughed as the door to the church opened.

Mick stared in shock as Erin walked down the aisle in a beautiful lace dress flanked by Wilma dressed in purple.

He still couldn't believe he had convinced her to get married. Not that he could claim all the credit. He had their friends to thank as well. It hadn't taken long for everyone to get over the scandal of Erin's past. They had held a big party for her when she finally qualified by completing her final exam.

The last six months had been a struggle in lots of ways. Getting Erin to completely trust herself, not to mention the rest of the world, had been challenging. She had finally decided to go back to medical school and gain her rightful qualifications.

While she was gone, he had plenty to do. Changing the Red Feathers into the Haven as well as unofficially adopting Michelle meant plenty of sleepless nights. The official adoption would happen once he and Erin were married. Lily had been a huge help. She had a real eye for interior design so he handed over the decoration of the house into her capable hands. The results were incredible. Instead of a gaudy old house, they now had a sedate residence decorated in creams and blues. It was very tasteful without a hint of red in sight.

Michelle's room was painted pink but that was allowed. Lily wouldn't let Michelle out of her sight so she doubled as her minder as well as doing the housekeeping duties. They had no guests as such yet although Mollie and her chaperone were staying with them for this week.

He smiled at Mollie who sat proudly in the front row with Michelle on her lap. Lily sat on one side and Wilma's friend, Harriet the lady from Santa Fe, sat on the other. Harriet had some ideas that might benefit the Haven. He looked forward to talking at length with her.

While Erin was away, they had corresponded by mail. The letters allowed them both the freedom to explore their most intimate thoughts. They were closer than ever.

* * *

Erin took a deep breath trying to steady her nerves. She loved Mick. She was certain of that but she couldn't help worrying the past would be repeated.

"Mick ain't a bit like your other husband. You got to put the past behind you, girl. Close that door and never let it open again."

"Yes, Wilma."

"You know I'm right but if ever you needed extra proof, why don't you open the wedding present he left for you?"

"Now? But the guests are waiting."

"Aw, let them wait. They might even say a few prayers while we all here." Wilma giggled but choked back the laughter at the look from Father Molloy.

Erin handed Wilma the flowers she was holding. She opened the package Mick had left at the orphanage that morning. It was a new shingle for the clinic. The brass plate was engraved with her name. Her new name.

Erin Quinn MD

"See, I told you he loves ya," Wilma whispered loud enough for everyone to hear.

The congregation laughed but Erin didn't care. Her gaze was locked with that of her future husband. She smiled as she read the promise of an amazing future. All she had to do was take the first step.

"Come on Wilma. I'm getting married."

* * *

FOR MORE IN the Clover Springs Series, click here.

IF YOU WOULD LIKE to read more about Doc Erin, Mick and their friends and how they cope with the 1888 Blizzard in New York try the Clover Springs East series.

ALSO BY RACHEL WESSON

The Resistance Sisters

Darkness Falls

Light Rises

Hearts at War

When's Mummy Coming

A Mother's Promise

WWII Irish Stand Alone

Stolen from her Mother

Orphans of Hope House

Home for unloved Orphans (Orphans of Hope House 1)

Baby on the Doorstep (Orphans of Hope House 2)

Women and War

Gracie under Fire

Penny's Secret Mission

Molly's Flight

Hearts on the Rails

Orphan Train Escape

Orphan Train Trials

Orphan Train Christmas

Orphan Train Tragedy

Orphan Train Strike

Orphan Train Disaster

Trail of Hearts - Oregon Trail Series

Oregon Bound (book 1)

Oregon Dreams (book 2)

Oregon Destiny (book 3)

Oregon Discovery (book 4)

Oregon Disaster (book 5)

12 Days of Christmas - co -authored series.

The Maid - book 8

Clover Springs Mail Order Brides

Katie (Book 1)

Mary (Book 2)

Sorcha (Book 3)

Emer (Book 4)

Laura (Book 5)

Ellen (Book 6)

Thanksgiving in Clover Springs (book 7)

Christmas in Clover Springs (book8)

Erin (Book 9)

Eleanor (book 10)

Cathy (book 11)

Mrs. Grey

Clover Springs East

New York Bound (book 1)

New York Storm (book 2)

New York Hope (book 3)

ACKNOWLEDGMENTS

These books wouldn't have been possible without the help of so many people. Thanks to Erin Dameron-Hill for my fantastic covers. Erin is a gifted artist who makes my characters come to life.

The ladies from Pioneer Hearts who volunteered to proofread my book. Special thanks go to Marlene Larsen, Cindy Nipper, Janet Lesley, Robin Malek, Meisje Sanders Arcuri and Denise Cervantes who all spotted errors that had slipped through.

Last, but by no means least, huge thanks and love to my husband and my three children.

Come join us at https://www.facebook.com/groups/rachelwessonsreaders

Printed in Great Britain
by Amazon

61598984R00160